Shadows and Solace

Blake Patrick

Dedication

To the silenced voices and the enduring spirits; to the stolen dreams and the unyielding courage; to the lost homes and the journeys uncharted—this book is dedicated to all those whose lives were forever altered by the Nazi regime.

To the generations that carry the weight of memories, to those who bear the legacy of resilience, this story honours your past and pledges to keep the flame of remembrance eternally alight.

May we never forget, may we always learn, and may we tirelessly work towards a world that upholds the dignity, equality, and sanctity of every human life.

FOR MORE INFORMATION, Contact blake.patrick.author@gmail.com
http://blake-patrick.co.uk

FIRST EDITION: OCTOBER 2023

Preface

In the somber annals of the 20th century, few events cast a longer shadow than the Holocaust. This book, "Shadows and Solace," is a work of fiction deeply rooted in the stark realities of that dark period, drawing upon the countless true stories of resilience, heartache, and the indomitable human spirit.

Within these pages lies the tale of Elsie and Karl, two individuals swept up in the tumultuous tide of World War II, whose paths converge in the most harrowing of places: Auschwitz. Their story is a poignant exploration of the depths of human cruelty and the incredible strength required not just to survive but to retain one's humanity amidst such brutality.

This narrative is an homage to the silent whispers, the hushed lullabies in the night, and the clandestine exchanges of hope that occurred between the walls of the concentration camps. It is a testament to the unspoken bonds formed in the face of shared suffering and the flickers of love that ignited in the all-consuming darkness.

As the author, I have tread carefully, mindful of the responsibility to honor the memory of those who lived through the horrors of the Holocaust. The characters of Elsie and Karl, while fictional, are composites of real experiences—echoes of the stories that have been entrusted to us by survivors, historians, and witnesses to the unthinkable.

"Shadows and Solace" is not just an account of survival against the odds. It is a narrative about the power of hope and the resilience of love.

It is a reminder that even when humanity seems lost, connection and compassion can still prevail.

As we turn the pages and step into the world of Elsie and Karl, let us do so with the understanding that while their story is a creation of fiction, the lessons it imparts are real and enduring. In remembering the past, we safeguard our future against the recurrence of such shadows, ensuring that the solace we find in our shared humanity remains ever-present.

With respect and reflection,
Blake Patrick

1

Whispers From The Past

The first golden rays of dawn streaked through the window, bringing warmth and light to the bustling city of Hamburg. In 1937, Hamburg, a bustling port city in Germany, found itself ensnared by the tightening grip of Nazi influence. The city's historic maritime prowess continued to thrive, with its port facilitating robust trade. Yet, beneath the façade of economic vigour, a darker transformation was underway. Swastikas adorned public spaces, and Nazi propaganda permeated daily life, casting shadows over the city's once-vibrant cultural tapestry. For Hamburg's Jewish community, the ominous weight of persecution loomed ever larger, with increasing discrimination and the foreboding presence of the Nuremberg Laws. Amidst this backdrop of political turbulence, the city's residents navigated a landscape of shifting allegiances, seeking solace where they could find it.

Elsie, with her chestnut hair cascading down her back, sat on the window sill of her apartment, overlooking the vibrant streets below. It was the spring of 1937, and the aroma of freshly baked pastries wafted up from the bakery on the ground floor, teasing her senses.

Elsie Zimmerman was born into the hum of Berlin's Roaring Twenties, a city where art and culture flourished against the backdrop of political unrest. Her father, a well-known conductor, instilled in her a passion for music that became the soundtrack of her early years, while her mother, a painter, introduced her to the vibrant strokes of art and color.

Elsie's childhood was a mosaic of piano recitals, art exhibitions, and the whispered excitement of a society on the brink of change. Her parents' liberal views and bohemian lifestyle shielded her from the grimmer realities outside their door, allowing her creativity and imagination to thrive.

As a teenager, Elsie's keen intellect and artistic talent earned her a place at Berlin's prestigious Bauhaus School. Here, she immersed herself in the avant-garde, rubbing shoulders with burgeoning artists and intellectuals. But as the decade drew to a close, the political landscape darkened. Elsie's vibrant world of expression and freedom began to be overshadowed by the rise of the Nazis.

In her early twenties, as Hitler came to power, Elsie watched in dismay as her vibrant city transformed. Friends fled, her family's works were denounced as "degenerate," and the joyous cacophony of Berlin's streets was replaced by the ominous march of boots.

A piano teacher by profession, Elsie adored the sounds and rhythms that encapsulated her world. The mornings were filled with the laughter of children and the soft, mellifluous notes that danced from her piano as she taught. Her afternoons were usually spent visiting the local park, where she'd often lose herself in a book or sketch the faces of strangers. She had a penchant for capturing moments, the essence of life on paper.

One of her drawings was of a young man she'd seen a few times at the park. With striking blue eyes and a disarming smile, Karl was hard to miss. Elsie didn't know him, but something about his demeanour, perhaps the way he lost himself while feeding the birds or playing the harmonica, made her want to capture him in her sketches.

In the bustling heart of Munich, Karl Becker was born into an era of dramatic shifts and intellectual fervor. His father, a professor of history, instilled in him an unquenchable thirst for knowledge and a deep appreciation for the power of the written word. His mother, a nurse who served in the Great War, imbued in him a sense of compassion and duty towards those in need.

Karl's youth was marked by an insatiable curiosity and a propensity for asking difficult questions. He grew up with his nose perpetually buried in newspapers, fervently debating current events with his father.

This passion for truth and storytelling naturally led him to a career in journalism.

After completing his studies at the University of Munich, where he honed his skills in rhetoric and writing, Karl took up a position at a local newspaper. He quickly garnered a reputation as a tenacious reporter, unafraid to tackle controversial topics. His columns, filled with fervor and insight, captured the turbulent spirit of the times.

As the political climate shifted with the rise of the Nazi party, Karl's work took on a new level of urgency. He witnessed firsthand the creeping censorship and propaganda that began to suffocate the press. Yet, he remained undeterred, using his articles to subtly critique the regime, weaving his dissent between the lines of seemingly innocuous stories.

It wasn't long before Karl's implicit criticisms caught the attention of the Gestapo. Friends and colleagues began to disappear, and the warnings became too frequent to ignore. It was during this time of heightened vigilance that he encountered Elsie. Her artistic soul and silent strength immediately drew him in, and together they became a beacon of silent rebellion.

But with each passing day, the danger grew closer, the shadows darker, and the choices starker. Karl knew the risks of his profession, but the truth was a siren call he could not resist. And it was this dedication to his craft, to the unveiling of lies and the presentation of facts, that led him down a path intertwined with Elsie's, straight into the heart of the story that would define their lives.

Karl, was a journalist for a local newspaper, having moved to Hamburg a year earlier. Passionate about unveiling truths and telling stories, he always carried his notepad and pen. Unknown to Elsie, he had noticed her too. Many times, he'd sit on a park bench opposite her, scribbling away, occasionally stealing glances in her direction. Karl admired the way she concentrated on her art, seemingly oblivious to the world around her.

His life was filled with ink stains and late nights at the news office. Journalism was more than just a job for Karl—it was his calling. He prided himself on digging deep, on revealing the heart of a story. His articles, often touching on the challenges faced by the common man amidst the changing political landscape, were well-loved and widely read.

Elsie's world was one of melodies, of delicate tunes that provided solace from the escalating tension outside her doors. In stark contrast, Karl's world was one of words, of harsh realities penned onto paper, stories that chronicled the disturbing winds of change in Germany.

Yet, amidst their contrasting worlds, their lives were destined to intertwine. One day, after months of silent admiration, their paths finally crossed. Elsie dropped her sketchbook, and the wind playfully tossed its pages around. Karl was quick to help her gather them.

"Thank you," Elsie whispered, her cheeks tinted with a faint blush.

"It's a pleasure," Karl responded, holding out the last page, the one with his sketch. "Seems I've caught your eye."

Elsie laughed, "You have an interesting face, perfect for practicing portraits."

They started meeting more often after that encounter, initially under the guise of 'art sessions' where Karl would pose, and Elsie would sketch. But soon, their meetings were filled with more than just art. They spoke about their dreams, fears, and the undercurrents of unease in their homeland.

Karl shared stories from his journalistic endeavours, often emphasizing the need for resilience and hope. "There's so much happening, Elsie. It's like a storm brewing on the horizon. We need to be the anchors for those around us."

Elsie, with her inherent optimism, always found a way to see the silver lining. "Every cloud has one, Karl. Even if the world around us is changing, we have our constants. Music, art, and stories."

It was evident that while the world outside grew colder and more unpredictable, Elsie and Karl found warmth in each other's company. They became each other's refuge.

As months turned into years, their bond deepened, and they became inseparable. Elsie introduced Karl to the world of music, and Karl introduced Elsie to the world of written words. They attended operas, visited art galleries, and even co-authored a series of articles on the cultural heart of Hamburg.

But as 1939 approached, the shadow of the impending war loomed large. The once-vibrant streets of Hamburg started to change. The music began to fade, replaced by hushed whispers and an undercurrent of fear. The political climate grew tense, and the familiar faces that Elsie and Karl once knew began disappearing.

One evening, as they sat in Elsie's apartment, listening to a record of Beethoven's Moonlight Sonata, Karl held her close. "Promise me, Elsie," he whispered, "that no matter what happens, you'll always remember these moments. The music, the laughter, the love."

Elsie nodded, tears glistening in her eyes. "Always, Karl. Always."

The world outside continued its descent into chaos, but for Elsie and Karl, these moments of love and serenity were their whispers from the past, a gentle reminder of a time when life was simpler, when hope was abundant, and when the melodies of love and life echoed louder than the drumbeats of war.

As the days turned into nights and nights into days, their meetings became more sporadic, filled with urgency and hushed tones. The newsroom where Karl worked was abuzz with the latest developments in Europe, and he often returned home exhausted, his face etched with lines of worry. The stories he wrote now bore a different tone—warnings, pleas, and unsettling reports about the rising power of the Nazi regime.

One evening, Elsie opened her door to find Karl standing there, his face pale, clutching a folded newspaper in his hand. Handing it to her, his fingers trembling slightly, he pointed to an article. It was one of his, an exposé on the brutalities being carried out against innocent citizens, especially those of Jewish heritage.

In an act of quiet defiance, Karl Becker penned an article that would resonate in the conscience of his readers. The piece, titled "In the Shadows of Progress: The Silent Voices of the Oppressed," was a masterful exposition of the brutalities inflicted upon innocent citizens under the guise of national rejuvenation and strength.

Karl began with a stark narrative, painting a vivid picture of the harsh realities on the streets of Germany. He detailed the plight of shopkeepers whose stores had been vandalized, of scholars ousted from academia, of musicians silenced by the banning of their art, and of entire families disappearing under the cloak of night.

He wrote with a poignancy that pierced through the numbing statistics, giving names and faces to the victims. Karl's prose was filled with an urgency that compelled the reader to see beyond the grand parades and soaring rhetoric of the Nazi regime.

The article subtly yet unmistakably criticized the government's actions, cloaked in enough allegory to pass the censors but clear enough for his audience to grasp its true meaning. He wove through his report the underlying theme of humanity's universal values being trampled upon, using historical parallels that drew on his father's teachings.

He ended the piece on a note that was both a call to action and a somber warning: "History's pages are often written in the ink of silence. Let us not allow the silence of our times to be the dark stains upon our nation's legacy."

Karl's article was a beacon of truth in a society increasingly shrouded in darkness. It was a testament to his courage as a journalist and his unwavering commitment to the principles of his profession. But little did he know, this article would set in motion events that would change his life forever.

"Elsie," he whispered hoarsely, "they didn't like it. My editor warned me to go into hiding."

Elsie's heart raced as she skimmed through the article, realizing the gravity of what Karl had penned and the danger he was now in. Her apartment, which had always been their sanctuary, suddenly felt vulnerable and exposed.

"We need a plan," she said, determination in her voice. "You can't stay here, and neither can I."

As the days progressed, the pair formulated a plan to leave Hamburg. Karl used his connections to procure forged documents while Elsie sold some of her most cherished possessions, including her beloved piano, to fund their escape.

But, as is often the case with best-laid plans, things didn't go smoothly. Rumours spread about the impending war, and borders tightened. Their attempts to leave were met with roadblocks at every turn.

As the grip of the regime tightened like a vice around Hamburg, Elsie and Karl were keenly aware that their window of opportunity to leave was rapidly closing. It wasn't just about their safety anymore; it was a race against time, a desperate bid for freedom before the borders sealed shut, trapping them within a nation succumbing to madness.

Their initial plan was simple and direct – to use the chaos of the increasingly frequent Allied bombings as a cover to slip away. But each time they tried, they found their paths blocked. Train stations were heavily monitored, with guards scrutinizing each passenger and demanding papers at gunpoint. Roads leading out of the city were often closed for "security reasons," or clogged with military traffic and refugees.

They considered alternate routes. The port, where ships still sailed out with precious cargo for the war effort, became a focal point of their strategy. Karl used his press credentials to gain information on ship departures, and Elsie leveraged her connections in the art world, many of whom were also seeking escape.

But here, too, they found insurmountable hurdles. The port was a hive of activity, swarming with officials and soldiers. Securing a spot on a ship required more than just stealth – it required complicity from officials, many of whom were ardent party supporters or too fearful of repercussions to offer aid.

Each failed attempt only served to heighten their sense of urgency. They witnessed the consequences of defiance – friends and acquaintances vanishing, only to be spoken of in hushed, fearful tones thereafter. The city they once knew, vibrant and bustling with life, was transforming into a prison of paranoia and suspicion.

In one final, desperate bid, they sought to escape through a network that helped political dissidents flee. This, too, proved fraught with danger. Informants and spies lurked in every corner, and the once-trusted network was riddled with leaks and traps. Their contact was arrested mere days before their planned departure, the safe house raided in the dead of night.

Each failed escape tightened the noose of despair around them. Yet, it was through these trials that Elsie and Karl's bond deepened. They shared not just a dream of freedom but now a profound understanding of the fragility of their situation. Their love became a sanctuary, a place of solace amid the growing storm.

In the end, their attempts to leave Hamburg were thwarted not by lack of will or planning but by a city and a regime that had turned against its own people. The roadblocks they met were physical manifestations of the insidious control the Nazis had exerted over Germany, a control that left little room for dissent or escape.

Their stolen moments were now tinged with an undercurrent of fear. They started meeting in secret locations, away from prying eyes. Elsie's sketches now were of maps, safe houses, and escape routes, while

Karl's writings were coded messages, warning their friends and seeking assistance.

One fateful evening, as they were planning their escape route in a dimly lit café, a familiar melody caught Elsie's ear. It was a song from her childhood, one her mother used to sing. The irony wasn't lost on her—the comforting tune juxtaposed against their grim circumstances.

Karl reached across the table, taking her hand. "Remember our promise," he whispered. "Always."

Elsie nodded, taking a deep breath, "Always."

Their bond grew stronger with each passing day, solidified by the adversities they faced. Despite the looming darkness, their love was the beacon that guided them, providing comfort in the most challenging times.

Weeks turned into months, and their plans became more desperate. They contemplated fleeing to neighbouring countries, but with each passing day, the Nazi influence grew, shutting down potential escape routes.

As the 1930s progressed, the Nazi influence over Hamburg became ever more pervasive and insidious. The city, renowned for its bustling port and cosmopolitan spirit, began to transform under the tightening grip of National Socialism.

INITIALLY, THE CHANGES were subtle. Flags adorned with the swastika started appearing on public buildings, and the streets began to host parades championing the Nazi ideology. The Hitler Youth and the League of German Girls became common sights, their uniforms and marching songs permeating the daily life of the city.

Local elections saw traditional parties sidelined by the National Socialist German Workers' Party, which began to dominate political discourse. Hamburg's Senate and government gradually filled with party members, ensuring that every aspect of civic life came under Nazi control. Laws were passed that marginalized Jewish citizens, and the once-vibrant political debates that characterized Hamburg's public life were replaced by a single, unchallenged voice—the voice of the Nazi regime.

Economically, businesses began to feel the pressure to align with the Nazis. Those that didn't were either boycotted or forcibly Aryanized, with Jewish-owned businesses being particularly targeted. The port, once a symbol of international trade and openness, became instrumental in the military buildup, as resources were increasingly diverted to support the Reich's expansionist aims.

Culturally, the city saw a crackdown on any form of expression deemed un-German. Books that didn't align with the party's ideologies were burned in public squares, artists were censored, and many intellectuals and creatives fled the country. The celebrated freedom of the Weimar era gave way to a culture of fear and propaganda, with the arts being harnessed to serve the state.

Socially, the fabric of Hamburg began to unravel as neighbors turned against neighbors. The Gestapo's presence was felt everywhere, and the ubiquitous informants made trust a scarce commodity. The persecution of Jews and other minorities intensified, with the establishment of the first anti-Jewish legislation and later, the horrifying pogroms that foreshadowed the Holocaust.

Education was not spared, as schools and universities were purged of 'undesirable' influences. A curriculum centered around racial purity, obedience to the Führer, and physical prowess replaced academic rigor and critical thinking. The indoctrination of the young became a central strategy for the Nazis, aiming to shape the next generation into loyal followers of the regime.

By the late 1930s, the Nazi influence in Hamburg was complete. The city was transformed into a bastion of National Socialism, with every street corner echoing the regime's rhetoric. The transformation was so profound that for those who remembered the Hamburg of old, it felt like an entirely different city—a city that had lost its soul to the shadows of tyranny.

As the whispers from the past became fainter and the present grew louder and more menacing, Elsie and Karl clung to their love, their dreams, and the hope that someday they would find their way back to the world they once knew—a world where love, art, and stories reigned supreme.

The two of them nestled in Elsie's apartment one last time, the world outside seemingly holding its breath, awaiting the storm that was about to descend.

2

DARKENING SKIES

HAMBURG, WITH ITS SPRAWLING ports and bustling streets, had always been a hub of activity, but by 1940, the atmosphere had shifted. The laughter and jovial conversations that once echoed through the streets had been replaced by hushed whispers and suspicious glances. The vibrancy of the city seemed dulled, overshadowed by a thick cloud of unease that hung in the air.

Shopfronts that once showcased the latest fashion, colourful toys, and delectable pastries, now often bore signs that read "No Jews Allowed." Neighbours who once greeted each other warmly began distancing themselves, not out of malice but fear. Even schools weren't spared, with children being indoctrinated with propaganda, their young minds moulded into instruments of the Nazi vision.

Elsie's piano lessons started dwindling. Parents, in fear of the ever-watching eyes of the Gestapo, refrained from engaging in any activity that might be deemed 'non-essential' or 'bourgeois'. The once harmonious notes that floated from her apartment became less frequent, replaced by the ominous broadcasts from radios detailing the greatness of the Reich.

Karl's journalism took a hit too. His newspaper, which once thrived on honest reporting, now operated under the oppressive thumb of the regime. Stories were censored, edited, or outright rejected if they didn't align with the Nazi propaganda. Many of Karl's colleagues, especially those of Jewish descent, started disappearing. They would either not show up for work, or there would be whispered conversations about them being 'relocated.'

One evening, as Elsie was returning from a rare piano lesson, she witnessed a scene that would forever be etched in her memory. A group of SA officers, often known as "Brownshirts," were the early paramilitary enforcers of the Nazi Party, instrumental in consolidating its grip on power and intimidating opposition, were publicly humiliating an elderly Jewish shopkeeper. They had painted the Star of David on his storefront and were forcing him to kneel and scrub it off, all the while jeering and laughing at his plight. The onlookers didn't intervene – some watched in silence, others in veiled horror, and a few even joined in the mockery.

Tears welled up in Elsie's eyes as she quickly turned the corner, trying to escape the cruel scene. When she reached her apartment, she bolted the door and sank to the floor, the weight of the world pressing heavily on her shoulders.

Karl, having faced his battles at the newspaper office, often visited Elsie to find solace. They would sit for hours, sometimes talking, sometimes just finding comfort in each other's presence. The reality outside was changing, and with it, their dreams and hopes.

One evening, Karl pulled out a stack of papers from his bag. They were articles, stories, and editorials that never made it to print, either censored by the regime or deemed too risky to publish.

"These are the truths, Elsie. The real stories of what's happening. Someday, the world needs to know," he murmured.

Elsie, taking the papers from him, gently said, "Then we'll be the keepers of these truths, Karl. We'll safeguard them until the world is ready to listen."

But as the days grew darker, so did the challenges they faced. Rationing began, with long queues for basic necessities becoming a common sight.

During World War II, rationing was a common practice, particularly in countries involved in the conflict, like Germany. The purpose of rationing was to ensure that scarce resources, such as food, clothing, and fuel, could be distributed equitably and conserved for the war effort.

In Hamburg, as in the rest of Germany, the rationing system was tightly controlled by the Nazi regime. The process was systematic and highly bureaucratic, involving several key steps:

Every citizen was issued a ration card, which was necessary to purchase certain items. These cards contained coupons that were specific to various types of goods. For example, there were separate coupons for meat, bread, sugar, and fats.

The amount of each item one could purchase was predetermined by the government and indicated on the ration card.

People were classified into groups based on their occupation, age, health, and importance to the war effort. Each group was allocated a different amount of rations. For instance, manual laborers and soldiers were allotted more substantial rations than office workers.

Rationed items were distributed through designated shops and centers. Individuals could only purchase their rations from the shop to which their card was registered.

When making a purchase, the shopkeeper would mark off the appropriate coupon on the customer's ration card

Certain groups, such as pregnant women, children, and the sick, were eligible for supplemental rations. These were often distributed through special channels, like hospitals or welfare organizations.

Despite the rationing system, a black market for goods flourished. Those with the means could obtain items illegally at a higher price.

Bartering became common, with individuals trading items they could spare for those they needed more.

Strict penalties were in place for hoarding or misusing ration coupons. The regime implemented severe punishments for violations to discourage any non-compliant behavior.

The rationing system, while designed to ensure fair distribution, often led to shortages and discontent among the population. In Hamburg, as the war progressed and resources became even scarcer, these rationing measures intensified, leading to increased hardship and hunger for the civilian population. It was a time marked by queues, scarcity, and a constant struggle to make do with what little was available.

The once-thriving port of Hamburg became a military stronghold, with ships carrying ammunition and soldiers instead of goods and traders.

Whispers of concentration camps, of mass relocations, and of extermination began to circulate.

As the 1930s progressed, unsettling rumors began to permeate through Europe. Whispers of concentration camps, mass relocations, and exterminations of Jews grew increasingly frequent and alarming. Initially, these tales were met with skepticism; they were too horrific, too monstrous to be believed. But as the decade drew to a close, the evidence became harder to ignore.

Word had leaked about the existence of concentration camps as early as the 1930s. Dachau, the first of these camps, was initially purposed for political prisoners, but as more camps were established, their scope broadened ominously. Escapees and released prisoners shared stories of brutal conditions, forced labor, and summary executions. While the full extent of the camps' purposes wasn't yet understood internationally, the rumors painted a grim picture of a regime willing to go to extreme lengths to silence and punish dissent.

The Nazi regime's policy of "relocating" Jews from their homes to ghettos and camps was initially framed as a form of "resettlement" for work and reeducation. However, as the war progressed, reports began to emerge from occupied territories of entire communities being uprooted, their homes and possessions confiscated. Trains packed with people were sent to unknown destinations. The forced relocation of Jews was not a secret, but the true nature and conditions of these ghettos and the fate of their inhabitants were shrouded in mystery and fear.

By the early 1940s, the most harrowing rumors had begun to surface: that the Nazis were systematically exterminating the Jewish population. These accounts were initially fragmentary and often arrived as faint signals through the fog of war. There were stories of mass shootings in the East, where Einsatzgruppen, mobile killing units, executed thousands of Jews in mass graves. With the implementation of the "Final Solution," the genocidal policy of the Nazi regime, more concrete information started to filter through. Reports from resistance fighters, Allied intelligence, and the few who managed to escape the camps all pointed to a systematic campaign of murder, involving gas chambers and crematoria.

The international response to these rumors was complex. Governments and individuals struggled to comprehend the scale and veracity of the reports. For many, there was a refusal to believe that such atrocities could occur in the 20th century. Others argued for action but faced bureaucratic hesitation and the fog of war. It wasn't until the liberation of the camps by Allied forces that the grim truth was laid bare for the world to see.

In places like Hamburg, where a semblance of normal life tried to persist amidst the war, these rumors circulated in hushed tones, fueling anxiety and dread among those who were at risk and guilt and complicity among those who chose to turn a blind eye. The very fabric of society seemed to be tearing at its seams.

Elsie's Jewish neighbours, the Rosenbergs, a kind elderly couple who had lived in Hamburg their whole lives, were taken away one night. Their apartment was sealed, and their possessions confiscated. The only reminder of their existence was a potted plant they had lovingly cared for, now wilting away on their balcony.

Karl, realizing the increasing danger of their situation, began making contingency plans.

Nestled within the maze of streets in Hamburg's old quarter stood a quaint bookshop, a relic from a bygone era of literary salons and philosophical debates. Its proprietor, an elderly bibliophile with a resistance leaner, had crafted within this unassuming shop a refuge for those like Karl, hunted and in dire need of sanctuary.

The bookshop was a labyrinth of shelves, each laden with volumes ranging from German classics to obscure poetry. The scent of aged paper and leather bindings filled the air, a fragrance that spoke of wisdom and worlds contained within words. In the far corner of the shop, behind a section dedicated to German romanticism, was the entrance to Karl's hidden attic abode.

To the untrained eye, the bookshelf appeared ordinary, indistinguishable from the countless others that lined the walls of the shop. However, the shelf was an ingenious creation, a façade that concealed the door to the attic. The shelf was hinged and fitted with a discreet locking mechanism that could be released by pulling a copy of Goethe's "Faust" – a symbol of the fight against darkness.

Upon releasing the lock, the shelf swung open, revealing a narrow staircase veiled in shadows. The ascent was steep and the steps creaked underfoot, a testament to the shop's venerable age. At the top was the attic – a modest space with a sloping roof and a small window that peeked out over the rooftops of Hamburg.

The attic was sparsely furnished. A small cot, a writing desk with a chair, and a lamp constituted the entirety of Karl's personal effects. The walls, though bare, were insulated with old newspapers and cloth to stave off the winter chill. A small stove in the corner provided warmth and allowed for the brewing of a clandestine cup of tea or coffee.

Here, in this hidden chamber of knowledge and resistance, Karl spent his days. The tranquil silence of the bookshop below was a sharp contrast to the heart-pounding terror that had become his constant companion. In this literary sanctuary, he continued to write, documenting the truths that the regime sought to suppress, his words a silent rebellion against the tyranny that sought to consume the world outside.

The bookshop, with its hidden attic, became a beacon of hope and a testament to human ingenuity and solidarity in the face of oppression. It was not just a hiding place but a stronghold of the human spirit, safeguarded behind the wisdom of Goethe and the countless authors who lined the shelves of the courageous bookshop.

One night, as the sirens wailed and the sounds of boots echoed in the streets, Karl and Elsie found themselves huddled in that attic. The dim candlelight revealed the fear in their eyes, but also the determination to survive.

"We must document everything, Elsie," Karl whispered, pulling out his notepad. "The world needs to know the truth."

And so, amidst the darkening skies, they began their secret mission. Elsie sketched scenes from their daily life - the ration queues, the public humiliations, the fearful faces. Karl wrote about the atrocities, the propaganda, and the stories of those who disappeared in the night.

As the days turned into weeks, and weeks into months, the couple clung to their love and their mission. They were no longer just bystanders to the events unfolding around them; they were chroniclers, documenting a world that was rapidly descending into chaos.

Every now and then, when the nights seemed unbearably long, and the sounds of distant gunfire served as a cruel lullaby, Karl would read out some of the tales he had penned. Stories of resilience, of people banding together, of little acts of kindness that shone brightly against the backdrop of darkness. And in return, Elsie would share her sketches, capturing raw emotions and stark realities.

During one of these nights, Elsie pulled out a particular sketch. It was of a young boy, no older than ten, handing out bread to those in line for rations. His eyes, though reflecting the weariness of the times, shone with hope and determination.

"I saw him yesterday," Elsie whispered. "In such bleak times, there are still rays of hope. Children, who despite everything, still find ways to be kind, to be human."

Karl nodded, brushing away a tear. "It's these stories, these moments, that give me hope. That even in the darkest of times, humanity will find its way back to the light."

They continued their secret documentation for months, using every scrap of paper, every drop of ink. Their work became a testament to a world gone awry, but also to the enduring human spirit that refused to be extinguished.

However, with every passing day, the risks grew higher. The Gestapo was intensifying their crackdowns, searching homes and businesses for dissenters and anyone deemed 'undesirable'. Friends and acquaintances began disappearing, their fates unknown.

One evening, a knock echoed through the bookshop. Karl and Elsie, hidden away in the attic, held their breaths as they heard muffled voices below. The door was forcefully opened, followed by the sound of boots trampling the wooden floors and books being thrown around. It was a raid.

The couple clung to each other, praying they wouldn't be discovered. As the minutes ticked by, the sounds grew closer, the footsteps echoing on the stairs leading to the attic. They prepared for the worst.

The resistance had long perfected the art of distraction, using cunning and chaos to divert the Gestapo's all-seeing eye. On the day they learned of the planned raid on the bookshop, a meticulous plan was quickly hatched. The group of fighters knew the stakes were high; the bookshop was not only Karl's sanctuary but a nexus for clandestine operations.

The ruse was to take place in the street directly adjacent to the bookshop, designed to draw the soldiers away just as they approached their target. A small cadre of resistance members, some disguised as market vendors and others as patrons, began their orchestrated commotion as the German patrol neared the shop.

A cart, laden with what appeared to be sacks of potatoes, was positioned at the street's narrowest point. On cue, as the German trucks rumbled closer, the cart's wheel "accidentally" buckled and snapped, spilling the contents across the cobblestones. The cart's owner, a wiry man with practiced theatrics, began a vociferous tirade, lamenting his misfortune and obstructing the soldiers' progress.

Simultaneously, another member of the resistance, feigning inebriation, stumbled into the scene, exacerbating the confusion with slurred songs and clumsy attempts to collect the scattered potatoes. A pair of women, resistance fighters masquerading as housewives, added to the pandemonium, scolding the "drunkard" and the cart owner with shrill voices that rose above the commotion.

As the soldiers attempted to clear the way, a couple of street urchins, coached by the resistance, darted through the legs of the crowd, snatching small items from the market stalls and sprinting away. This prompted several vendors to give chase, shouting for the military police to intervene. The orchestrated chaos swelled like a symphony, each participant playing their part to perfection, drawing the soldiers' attention and resources.

Amidst the bedlam, smoke began to billow from a nearby alleyway, further adding to the confusion. Someone had set fire to a pile of refuse, sending up clouds of thick, choking smoke that wafted towards the crowd. The strategically lit fire was small but produced enough smoke to cause alarm and obscure vision.

With the soldiers now distracted by the task of crowd control, fire extinguishing, and petty theft, the resistance fighters near the bookshop sprang into action. Using the uproar as cover, they signaled Karl and Elsie to flee through the back, where a motorcycle waited in the alley for a quick getaway. Meanwhile, inside the shop, other members of the resistance swiftly concealed any incriminating evidence.

The diversion, a cacophony of calculated chaos, was a resounding success. By the time the German soldiers realized the extent of their misdirection, Karl and Elsie had vanished into the city's warren of backstreets, and the bookshop stood as just another quiet store on a street now calm. The resistance had once again outwitted the Gestapo, proving that in the shadow of oppression, the light of ingenuity and solidarity burned all the brighter.

"We can't stay in the attic any longer," Karl whispered, looking at the Elsie. "It's only a matter of time before they come back."

Elsie nodded, clutching the bundle of sketches and writings they had created. "Wherever we go, we take these with us. The world needs to remember."

The couple, under the cover of darkness, set out on a new journey, leaving behind the familiar streets of Hamburg. The skies might have darkened, but their mission, their purpose, was crystal clear. They would be the bearers of truth, the whisperers of stories that needed to be told.

3

THE INEVITABLE

The maze of narrow alleyways and old brick walls of Hamburg once provided a solace and familiarity to both Karl and Elsie, but with the Gestapo's ever-watching eyes, these lanes now seemed like a trap, ready to ensnare them at any given moment.

Karl had become a wanted man, not only for his past journalistic endeavours but also because of his association with known members of the resistance. He knew he was being hunted, and every step he took was weighed down by the knowledge that it could be his last as a free man. He'd taken to using pseudonyms, moving frequently from one safe house to another, always a step ahead of his pursuers—or so he hoped.

One fog-laden evening, as he made his way to a safe house on the outskirts of the city, he felt an odd sensation, like he was being watched. Pausing briefly to light a cigarette, he tried to shake off the feeling. But as he exhaled, hands grabbed him from behind, pulling him into the shadows. Before he could react, a cloth covered his mouth, and the world faded into darkness.

Elsie, on the other hand, continued to reside in Hamburg, always under a cloud of anxiety for Karl but trying to maintain some semblance of normalcy. She had shifted her focus from teaching piano to nursing, working at a local hospital. Here, she saw the horrors of war first-hand: soldiers with life-altering injuries, civilians traumatized by the brutality they had witnessed, and children orphaned by the conflict.

While her medical knowledge was limited, her ability to offer solace, to be a calming presence amidst the storm, made her indispensable. It also made her privy to information—whispers of upcoming raids, lists of those targeted, and sometimes even covert messages from the resistance.

One evening, after a particularly gruelling shift, as Elsie was heading home, she was stopped by two officers. They demanded her papers, scrutinizing them under the dim streetlight.

"We've had reports of suspicious activities in the hospital," one of the officers growled. "And we have reason to believe you're involved."

Before she could protest, she was forcefully taken to a waiting vehicle, her pleas falling on deaf ears.

Karl awoke in a dimly lit cell, his head pounding. The cold stone floor was unforgiving, and the bars on the tiny window allowed only a sliver of light. The stench of despair permeated the air. Whispers from adjoining cells spoke of torture, of forced confessions, and of disappearances. Time seemed to stretch indefinitely, with days blurring into nights.

In the grip of the Gestapo, Karl found himself in the bowels of a building that was as cold and unyielding as the hearts of the men who roamed its hallways. The interrogation room was stark, its walls bare except for the peeling grey paint that seemed to mirror the grim reality of Karl's situation. A single bulb hung from the ceiling, casting more shadows than light.

Across from Karl sat Jurgen Daluege, an officer whose reputation for cruelty was whispered about even amongst his fellow Nazis. Daluege's methods were known to be ruthless, not for their physicality but for their ability to break a man's spirit. His face was impassive, giving nothing away, his eyes fixed on Karl with a predator's intensity.

The questions began like a metronome, steady and relentless. Karl's journalistic instincts, which had always served him well in seeking truth, now became his shield. He crafted his answers with care, revealing nothing of substance, protecting his comrades and the resistance efforts with every non-answer and diversion.

Daluege's tactics shifted like quicksilver. He would lean back in his chair, feigning boredom with Karl's responses, only to lean forward abruptly, invading Karl's personal space in an attempt to unnerve him.

He employed silence as a weapon, letting the quiet stretch on until it was heavy with anticipation, waiting for Karl to fill it with the confessions he sought.

Hours turned into days, and Karl's sense of time began to warp. He was returned to his cell between sessions, each time more exhausted, his mind reeling from the psychological barrage. The cell offered no comfort, its cold stone floor and the thin blanket provided little respite from the chill that seemed to seep into his bones.

Food was scarce, a meager loaf of bread and some water, and sleep was a fickle ally, coming in fitful bursts between the echoes of distant screams and the constant clinking of chains. Karl held fast to the image of Elsie, her strength, and her courage serving as his beacon through the dark hours. He replayed every moment they had shared, every quiet act of rebellion, every whispered promise of a future free from tyranny.

Back in the interrogation room, Daluege's tactics escalated. He began to bring in objects from Karl's past—his typewriter, a scarf Elsie had worn, articles he had written—placing them on the table between them as if they were pieces in a cruel game. "We know more than you think," Daluege would insinuate, his voice a low, threatening drawl.

Yet, Karl remained a fortress of resolve. Despite the isolation, the hunger, and the mind games, he gave away nothing. Daluege, growing increasingly frustrated with Karl's resilience, began to weave elaborate lies, telling Karl that Elsie had been captured, that his resistance friends had all confessed and named him as the leader. Each falsehood was designed to chip away at Karl's defenses, to exploit the emotional cracks that Daluege was sure must exist.

But Karl knew better. He understood the game of doubt and deception being played against him. He clung to the one truth he knew—the love and loyalty that bound him and Elsie together, the shared commitment to their cause that was stronger than any of Daluege's manipulations.

Daluege, sensing that his usual methods were bearing no fruit, changed his approach once more. He became almost cordial, offering Karl cigarettes and better food, feigning concern for his well-being. "You're a smart man, Karl," he would say. "Why waste your life for a lost cause? Cooperate, and you can have a future."

Karl, however, saw through the veneer of kindness. He knew that this, too, was just another form of torture, a psychological ploy aimed at breaking him down. He held steadfast, drawing on an inner well of fortitude he hadn't known he possessed.

Elsie's time at the detention center was a period marked by a chilling routine, one that stripped away the freedoms and dignities she once knew. Upon arrival, she was processed with cold efficiency. Her personal effects were confiscated, and her identity was reduced to a number stamped onto coarse fabric. The person who had once been Elsie Zimmerman, the artist and the dreamer, was now just another face in the crowd of the detained.

Her days were structured and monotonous. Wake-up calls came before dawn, rousing the detainees from their restless sleep for roll call. They were made to stand in rigid lines, regardless of the weather, while guards counted and recounted, often using this as an opportunity to exert their authority through random acts of cruelty.

The living quarters were cramped and unsanitary. Elsie and other women were packed into small cells that allowed for neither privacy nor comfort. The bunk beds, stacked three high, had thin, lumpy mattresses that did little to cushion the hard metal frames. Each morning, she folded her thin blanket meticulously, a small act of defiance to maintain some order in a world that had descended into chaos.

Meals were sparse and provided at irregular intervals. The food, often just a thin soup and a piece of stale bread, was hardly enough to sustain the labor that was demanded of them. Elsie, once used to the warmth of a family kitchen and the shared meals with friends, now found herself swallowing her ration in silence, often under the watchful and unsympathetic gaze of the guards.

The work assigned to her was grueling and seemingly without purpose, designed to wear down the prisoners both physically and mentally. Some days, it was moving heavy stones from one place to another, and on others, it was scrubbing floors until her knuckles turned raw and her back ached. The futility of the work was a psychological tactic, meant to break the spirit of those who were detained.

In the evenings, after their labors, the women were often left to their own devices. This time could have offered a respite, but instead, it became a vacuum filled with anxiety and dread. Whispers of what lay beyond the detention center's walls—the transport to work camps or worse—circulated among the detainees. Fear was a constant companion, its icy grip unrelenting.

Throughout it all, Elsie maintained a semblance of hope. She would gather with other women, sharing stories of better days and singing softly to keep their spirits alive. They would speak in hushed tones of news from the outside, of the resistance, and of the potential for liberation, though such discussions were always fraught with risk.

The detention center, with its barbed wire and watchtowers, became a place where time seemed to stand still, and where the world outside felt both impossibly close and hopelessly out of reach. For Elsie, it was a time of endurance, of clinging to the memories of who she once was, and of hoping for the chance to be that person once again.

But amidst the torment, there were fleeting moments of humanity. An older prison guard, perhaps reminded of his daughter when he looked at Elsie, would occasionally slip her a piece of bread or allow her a few minutes in the courtyard to feel the sun on her face.

Days turned into weeks. Both Karl and Elsie, in their separate prisons, clung to memories of their time together—the stolen moments, the shared dreams, and the promise they had made to each other. The memories became a beacon, a source of strength in their darkest hours.

One evening, as Elsie was being returned to her cell after yet another gruelling interrogation, she overheard two guards discussing a planned mass transfer of prisoners to a camp further east. The name resonated with terror: Auschwitz.

Despair gripped her heart, but she also felt a spark of determination. She began discreetly gathering information, listening to whispered conversations, and noting the routines of the guards. If there was even the slightest chance of escape, she was determined to take it.

Similarly, Karl, using his journalistic instincts, began piecing together fragments of information. He learned of the extermination camps and the grim fate that awaited many. Using charred bits of wood from his cell, he started documenting his experiences, hiding the notes in the cracks of the cell walls, hoping that someday, someone would find them.

Both Elsie and Karl, unbeknownst to each other, were being loaded onto transport trains bound for the same destination. The transport train to Auschwitz was a claustrophobic nightmare for Elsie, Karl, and the countless others crammed into its confines. These cattle cars, designed for freight rather than human passengers, were suffocatingly overcrowded, with people pressed against one another, devoid of adequate ventilation. The air inside was thick, fetid with the stench of sweat, fear, and waste. There was no space to sit, let alone lie down, forcing many to stand for the journey's excruciating duration. The barest slits served as windows, letting in scant light but no fresh air. Food and water were in pitifully short supply, and the sanitary conditions were non-existent, with no facilities for relief. The constant rattling of the train combined with the moans of despair and cries of children created an unending cacophony, a grim prelude to the horrors of Auschwitz. Every rattle of the train tracks, every mournful whistle of the engine, only served to amplify the uncertainty of what lay ahead.

Inside the carriage, people were packed like sardines, their faces a canvas of despair, confusion, and grief. Children clung to their parents, their innocent eyes wide with fear. The elderly, some frail and on the brink of giving up, whispered prayers and tried to comfort the younger ones.

Elsie found herself next to a young mother with a baby, its soft cries barely audible above the din. She offered to hold the infant, trying to soothe it with lullabies she remembered from her own childhood. The mother, grateful for the small reprieve, rested her head against the wooden panel, tears streaming down her face.

Karl, on the other hand, was in a carriage further down. He tried to strike up conversations with his fellow prisoners, hoping to glean any information about their destination or the resistance's activities. Among them was a teacher, a baker, a doctor—all ordinary people who had found themselves caught in the crossfire of an extraordinary and devastating situation.

As the journey continued, the conditions in the carriages deteriorated. With no access to food, clean water, or sanitation facilities, sickness began to spread. The air grew thick with despair.

One evening, as the train trundled through a dense forest, it came to a sudden halt. The doors were thrown open, and guards shouted orders, their voices cold and devoid of empathy. Karl, using the chaos as a cover, managed to scribble a note, entrusting it to a young boy who seemed to be part of a larger family group. "Find Elsie," he whispered, giving a brief description of her. "Tell her to stay strong. Tell her I love her."

As the prisoners were herded out, the vast expanse of the camp came into view. The infamous sign, "Arbeit macht frei" (Work sets you free), loomed overhead, a cruel irony to the reality of the camp. A suffocating blanket of terror enveloped Elsie and Karl. The camp's looming barbed wire fences and austere watchtowers immediately conveyed an inescapable sense of doom. The air was thick with the acrid scent of smoke, hinting at unspeakable horrors. Loud, harsh commands in German pierced the air, accompanied by the menacing barks of guard dogs. The immediate separation of families and the systematic dehumanization processes, like shaving of heads and tattooing of numbers, deepened their despair. They could hear distant cries and sobs, each a testament to a broken spirit. The camp's stark environment, coupled with whispered rumours of gas chambers and relentless exterminations, intensified the dread. For Elsie and Karl, Auschwitz was not just a place; it epitomized the darkest abyss of humanity, where hope was the rarest of commodities.

Separated by gender, Elsie and Karl were processed and assigned to different parts of the camp. But amidst the overwhelming terror and confusion, a small beacon of hope emerged—the young boy managed to find Elsie. Handing her the crumpled note, he relayed Karl's message.

Elsie, her eyes brimming with tears, clutched the note to her heart, drawing strength from Karl's words. The journey ahead was uncertain, filled with challenges and heartbreak, but knowing that Karl was nearby, that their love remained unbroken, gave her the courage to face the inevitable horrors that awaited.

The arrival at Auschwitz was a descent into an abyss that Elsie and Karl could never have imagined. Herded from the cattle cars after enduring the seemingly endless journey, they were met with the cacophony of shouting guards, barking dogs, and the cries of the disoriented and frightened. The infamous archway loomed overhead, its deceitful promise of 'work bringing freedom' was a grim omen of the lie they were walking into.

The initial processing was a blur of commands and confusion. Separated by gender, Elsie and Karl could only exchange fleeting, terrified glances before being swallowed by the crowd. Elsie was pushed along with a sea of women towards a stark, grey building ominously referred to as 'the showers.' The air was thick with the mix of fear and the industrial scent of the camp.

Stripped of their belongings, their hair shorn, and their identities reduced to numbers, the final shred of their past lives was taken when they were forced to undress. The room was cold and clinical, with its concrete floors and walls that echoed with the sound of their captors' indifferent instructions. The naked vulnerability of the group was profound, as they huddled together for warmth and a modicum of privacy.

The uncertainty was the cruelest part. Rumors of gas chambers masquerading as showers had filtered through the collective consciousness of European Jewry, and each of them was acutely aware of this as they were prodded towards their potential death. The fear was palpable, a visceral entity that clung to their skin more tightly than the clothes they had just shed.

As they were herded into the shower room, a silence descended. Eyes closed, prayers whispered, goodbyes thought to loved ones, and hearts pounding so fiercely they threatened to break ribs. Every second stretched into eternity as they waited for water or death to rain down from the showerheads above.

And then, water – cold and biting, but water nonetheless – began to pour. Relief flooded in brief waves, though it did little to warm their chilled bodies or soothe their shattered spirits. For now, death had passed them by, but the relief was tainted, for they knew that survival in Auschwitz meant the continual looming of its possibility, with each day bringing its own form of despair and dehumanization.

For Elsie and Karl, this would be the first of many horrors they would have to endure, a constant cycle of fear, relief, and the unyielding pressure to maintain hope amidst the hopelessness that had become their reality.

4

HELL ON EARTH

A chilling wind swept across the vast expanse of Auschwitz, as Elsie, along with hundreds of others, was herded through the iron gates. The vastness of the camp, with its imposing watchtowers, electrified fences, and the endless rows of barracks, was a terrifying sight to behold.

Karl, on the other hand, had been directed to a separate section of the camp. As he marched, his gaze searched the sea of faces for Elsie, hoping against hope that he might catch a glimpse of her. But with every passing moment, the weight of their separation grew heavier.

Inside the camp, the prisoner sheds stood as grim reminders of the systematic dehumanization the inmates endured. These structures, originally designed for military use or even as stables, were ill-suited for human habitation, especially given the overcrowded conditions the Nazis imposed.

The wooden bunks, stacked three or four high, offered no mattresses or pillows. Instead, prisoners found themselves sleeping on rough, splintered planks, packed tightly with multiple individuals sharing a single, narrow space. These sleeping conditions, exacerbated by the infestations of lice and rats, made rest a fleeting luxury. The lack of adequate insulation within these sheds ensured that the biting cold of winter and the stifling heat of summer were felt in their extremes.

Sanitation facilities were shockingly inadequate. The few available latrines were perpetually overflowing and were cleaned infrequently, contributing to the pervasive, nauseating stench that clung to the sheds. Fresh water was a rarity, with prisoners often resorting to drinking from muddy puddles or collecting rainwater, when they could find it.

Meal times brought little relief. The food, often just a watery soup with occasional floating bits of vegetable or meat, was neither nutritious nor filling. It was distributed in communal bowls, and the ensuing scramble for sustenance often led to further humiliations and scuffles.

Amidst this squalor, the prisoners tried to find solace where they could. A shared scrap of bread, a whispered word of encouragement, or a covertly shared story became their lifelines. But the omnipresent threat of random violence from the guards, combined with the ever-looming spectre of disease and malnutrition, made the sheds of Auschwitz a living nightmare for Elsie, Karl, and thousands like them.

The first days were a blur of roll calls, meagre rations, and forced labour. Prisoners, already weak and emaciated, were pushed to their limits, their every move watched by guards with a penchant for cruelty.

In Auschwitz, where the struggle for survival was constant and the line between life and death perilously thin, prisoners engaged in various forms of resourcefulness to improve their dire circumstances. These acts of cunning were not only a means to endure but also served as quiet forms of resistance against the dehumanizing conditions imposed upon them.

Knowledge was a valuable commodity, and in defiance of the Nazis, clandestine classes were held. Learned prisoners taught others in secret, sharing knowledge of literature, history, and languages. These covert lessons were a way to maintain a sense of identity and humanity.

Prisoners learned to barter and trade for better rations or items that could improve their living conditions. A piece of bread might be traded for a warmer pair of socks, or a valued skill such as shoemaking might be exchanged for extra food.

Some prisoners attempted to cultivate relationships with the guards or kapo for better treatment. They might offer up a talent, like playing an instrument or drawing, in exchange for less grueling work assignments or an additional ration of food.

Where possible, prisoners created small hidden gardens to grow extra food, such as potatoes or onions. They also became adept at foraging for edible plants during work details outside the camp's main perimeter.

Prisoners learned to hoard bits of food when they could. They created hidden pockets in their clothing or found loose bricks or cracks in their sleeping quarters to hide away a small stash for days when the rations were even less than usual.

To stave off the cold, prisoners would improvise extra layers of clothing. They unraveled threads from their bedding to knit into gloves or stuffed paper into their clothes for insulation.

For many, maintaining spiritual and religious practices provided psychological comfort. They would secretly observe rituals and holidays, often with improvised items, to retain a sense of faith and hope.

In the face of despair, creating art or making music became acts of rebellion. Prisoners composed songs, wrote poetry, and even crafted makeshift instruments, which allowed brief escapism from their grim reality.

Understanding the link between cleanliness and disease, prisoners went to great lengths to maintain personal hygiene. They used scraps of cloth as washcloths or toothbrushes and carefully collected and used any water they could find for washing.

Perhaps most importantly, prisoners formed tight-knit communities to provide emotional support to one another. They shared stories of their lives before the war, offered shoulders to cry on, and formed bonds that went beyond the mere need for survival.

Each of these acts, small in isolation, became part of a larger tapestry of resilience. The prisoners of Auschwitz demonstrated remarkable ingenuity and courage, finding ways to uplift one another and maintain a semblance of dignity in a place designed to strip them of it entirely.

Elsie, due to her previous nursing experience, was assigned to the camp's infirmary— The infirmary, or "Revier" as it was often referred to in the camp, stood as an ironic structure within Auschwitz. It was supposed to be a place of healing amidst the horrors, but often it became another instrument of death, with selections and lethal injections being commonplace. Yet for Elsie, working there was a grim privilege—it offered a slight reprieve from the external hard labour and provided opportunities, albeit limited, to offer compassion in a place where humanity was scarce.

Elsie's day began before dawn, awakened by the stern voice of a Kapo or an SS guard, ensuring every inmate was accounted for. Following a brief and often cold breakfast, she would make her way to the infirmary, a hurried journey made in the dim early light.

Once inside, she was assigned tasks by the medical personnel, which sometimes included actual doctors but were often comprised of prisoner-doctors or even inmates with little to no medical training. The 'patients' brought in were a harrowing sight—men and women with swollen limbs, open wounds, frostbites, and the ghostly pallor of malnutrition and disease.

Most of Elsie's tasks were rudimentary but essential. She was responsible for changing bandages, a job that might sound simple but was made challenging by the lack of supplies. Often, bandages were washed, dried, and reused, with Elsie trying her best to ensure they were as clean as possible to prevent further infections.

Another part of her day was spent assisting with surgeries. With no anesthesia, these procedures were agonizing for the patients. Elsie's role was to hold down the struggling patients and offer words of comfort, trying to soothe their pain with hushed lullabies or whispered reassurances.

Cleaning the infirmary was a never-ending task. With only rudimentary supplies, Elsie, alongside other inmates, scrubbed the floors, cleaned the rudimentary surgical instruments, and tried to maintain a semblance of sanitation in the grim surroundings.

Lunch was brief, often taken on the go. The infirmary staff were sometimes given slightly better rations, a cruel incentive by the Nazis to keep the workers there motivated. However, even these 'better' meals were woefully inadequate.

Amidst the tangible horrors, Elsie also became an emotional pillar for many. She listened to the whispered stories of the infirm, holding the hands of those too weak to speak, offering a shoulder to cry on or a brief, comforting embrace.

The evening brought its own challenges. The infirmary was also where the SS would conduct selections, deciding who would live to see another day and who would be sent to the gas chambers. Elsie, trying to stay invisible during these selections, would often find herself shepherding the selected inmates, offering words of solace or, when possible, sneaking them a piece of bread or a sip of water.

As night fell and she made her way back to her own barrack, Elsie's heart bore the heavy weight of the day's events. But amidst the pain, she also carried with her the small victories—the grateful smile of a healed inmate, the whispered 'thank you' from a comforted soul, or the silent camaraderie shared with fellow infirmary workers. In a world where darkness prevailed, these were her slivers of light.

Every morning, even before the sun dared to pierce the sombre gray skies of Auschwitz, the shrill blare of a whistle disrupted the fragile sleep of the camp inmates. For Karl, like many others, this signalled the beginning of yet another gruelling day of forced labour.

After a rushed roll call, where prisoners stood in rigid lines regardless of the weather, awaiting the meticulous count of the guards, Karl and his assigned group were marched off to their work site. They were accompanied by SS guards, their rifles always at the ready, and occasionally, snarling dogs strained at their leashes, eager to be unleashed at the slightest sign of dissent.

Karl was assigned to a group that worked on road construction. The Nazis, aiming to enhance the infrastructure surrounding the camp, required roads for better transportation of goods and more prisoners. The work was back-breaking. Armed with rudimentary tools, the prisoners had to first clear any existing terrain—this meant removing trees, shrubs, and rocks, often with their bare hands. The heavy stumps and boulders, resistant to their exhausted attempts, had to be dragged away, sometimes requiring the strained effort of several men.

Once cleared, the next task was to level the ground. This often involved shifting large quantities of earth, creating embankments where needed. The physical exertion was immense. The prisoners worked without protective gear, their thin camp uniforms offering little protection against sharp stones, splinters, or the elements.

After the ground was prepared, the laying of stones began. These stones, meant to form the road's foundation, were often sourced from nearby quarries. Karl, on more than one occasion, was also part of a team sent to extract these stones. Swinging heavy pickaxes and then manually breaking down the extracted rocks to the required size was tedious and physically draining.

Lunch breaks were short and provided little respite. The meagre ration of watery soup was consumed quickly, with prisoners huddled together, seeking warmth and sharing whispered conversations. After this brief pause, the labour resumed, continuing until dusk began to fall.

The return to the camp in the evening was a march of the utterly exhausted. Every muscle in Karl's body would scream in protest, his hands bearing the raw blisters of his toils, and his face caked in a mix of sweat and dirt. Yet, the day's end brought no immediate relief. On reaching the camp, there was another roll call, often longer than the morning's, with guards taking perverse pleasure in their power, making the prisoners stand for hours.

Finally, when released to their sheds, Karl and his fellow inmates would collapse onto their hard bunks, trying to find a few hours of rest before the cruel cycle began again. Amidst this punishing routine,

Karl's thoughts often wandered to Elsie, drawing strength from their shared dreams of a life beyond the barbed wires.

It was during the morning roll-call that Karl first encountered Oberst Heinz, the camp commandant. Oberst Friedrich Heinz grew up in a world far removed from the concentration camps' cruel confines. Born in 1899 in a small German town to a middle-class family, he experienced the pride of German nationalism early in his life. His father, a World War I veteran, filled young Heinz's ears with tales of battlefield valour and the importance of upholding German honour. But along with these tales of valour came tales of resentment, especially concerning the Treaty of Versailles and the perceived humiliations it imposed on Germany.

During his formative years, Heinz was fed a steady diet of anti-Semitic propaganda, often hearing about how the Jews were to blame for Germany's post-war economic troubles and societal ills. This narrative was further reinforced in the local schools he attended, where nationalistic fervour was entwined with academic pursuits.

As he matured, Heinz gravitated towards the burgeoning National Socialist German Workers' Party. The Nazi ideologies resonated with his deeply ingrained beliefs. Climbing the ranks quickly due to his fierce loyalty and ruthless demeanour, Heinz became a trusted member of the SS. His unquestioning adherence to the Party's anti-Semitic principles combined with his tactical skills made him an ideal candidate for overseeing concentration camps.

Auschwitz, with its harrowing reputation, became his dominion. Heinz, now Oberst, viewed his role not just as a duty, but as a divine mission to cleanse the Aryan race of its impurities. This dehumanization of Jews, in his eyes, was not a matter of personal animosity but a twisted sense of righteousness.

His brutality towards Jewish prisoners wasn't just rooted in the systemic anti-Semitism of the Nazi regime, but also in a deeply personal vendetta. Early in his military career, Heinz believed he was undermined by a Jewish superior officer, which stunted his initial rise within the ranks. This incident, minor as it might have been, left a lasting scar on Heinz's psyche, fuelling his hatred and need for retribution.

Within Auschwitz, he ruled with an iron fist. He viewed any sign of resistance, no matter how small, as a direct affront to his authority and the Nazi mission. His fury wasn't limited to physical violence; he also relished in psychological torment, using fear as a tool to break the prisoners' spirits.

Yet, like many tyrants, Oberst Heinz was also plagued by insecurities. He was haunted by nightmares and constantly feared retribution. He used brutality as a shield, hoping that the sheer scale of his atrocities would deter any would-be avengers. But deep inside, the weight of his actions bore down on him, though he'd never admit it, even to himself.

In a world that often seeks simplistic explanations for the cruelty of figures like Oberst Heinz, the truth is frequently more complex. He was a product of his upbringing, societal influences, personal vendettas, and psychological frailties, all converging to create the monster that ruled Auschwitz with unrelenting cruelty.

One day, during the roll call, a frail old man collapsed from exhaustion. Without a moment's hesitation, Oberst Heinz, who happened to be present, spurred his horse forward and, with a cruel smirk, trampled the old man underfoot. The message was clear: weakness would not be tolerated.

Word of Oberst Heinz's cruelty quickly spread throughout the camp. Whispers among the prisoners told of his twisted games, where he would force prisoners to inflict pain on one another for his entertainment. Those who refused would meet even grimmer fates.

Elsie heard these tales in the infirmary, as she tended to the wounds both visible and hidden. One day, a young woman named Lina, trembling and in tears, recounted her encounter with Heinz. She had been handpicked, along with a few others, to dine with him at his quarters. The evening had started with a semblance of civility, but as the night wore on, Heinz's true nature emerged. The women were humiliated, tormented, and some even subjected to unspeakable acts of violence.

As Lina confided in Elsie, the weight of her trauma evident in her eyes, Elsie felt a surge of rage. She had witnessed the depths of human cruelty in the camp, but the sadistic pleasure Heinz derived from his acts was a new level of evil.

Karl, meanwhile, had his own encounter with the infamous commandant. One day, as he was working on repairing a section of the fence, he accidentally dropped a tool just beyond the perimeter. Knowing the consequences of attempting to retrieve it, he decided to leave it. But fate had other plans.

Oberst Heinz, who had been observing from a distance, sauntered over, a malicious grin on his face. "Is this how you repay the generosity of the Reich?" he sneered, pointing at the tool. "Retrieve it."

Karl hesitated. Stepping beyond the fence, even with Heinz's order, was a death sentence. The electrified barrier had claimed many lives. But Heinz's cold gaze left no room for defiance. Taking a deep breath, Karl reached out, his fingertips just grazing the tool. In that split second, Heinz, with a swift move, pushed Karl against the fence. The shock threw Karl several feet back, his body convulsing from the electric jolt.

Laughter echoed from Heinz as he turned on his heels and walked away, leaving Karl writhing in pain on the ground. Fellow prisoners rushed to his aid, dragging him to safety. The scars from the incident, both physical and psychological, would remain with Karl for a long time.

As days turned into weeks, the horrors of Auschwitz became a grim reality for Elsie and Karl. But amidst the despair, a sliver of hope remained. They both clung to the memories of their time together, drawing strength from their love, and praying that they would one day be reunited. At the evening roll call, where the prisoners were lined up in rows, their faces a testament to the weariness and suffering they endured. The sun cast long shadows, painting the camp in hues of orange and red.

Oberst Heinz stood on an elevated platform, his presence dominating the scene. He read out numbers—prisoner numbers—and with each call, a life was upended. Those called were destined for 'special duties', a term that, in the hellish landscape of Auschwitz, could mean anything from lethal experiments to gas chambers.

Elsie, standing in line, tried to focus on the horizon, hoping to catch a glimpse of the area where Karl was stationed. But with the camp's vastness and the sea of prisoners, it was like searching for a needle in a haystack.

Suddenly, a commotion broke out a few rows ahead. A prisoner had collapsed, his strength finally giving out. Guards rushed in, batons raised, ready to mete out punishment. But to Elsie's horror, she recognized the man—it was Karl.

Heart pounding, she broke ranks and rushed forward, her only thought to reach him. The guards, taken aback by her audacity, momentarily hesitated. Oberst Heinz, observing from his platform, signalled for them to hold back.

As Elsie reached Karl, she cradled his head in her lap, her tears falling on his dirt-streaked face. Their reunion, amidst the grim backdrop of Auschwitz, was a heart-wrenching scene, their love a stark contrast to the cruelty that surrounded them.

Oberst Heinz, intrigued by this display of emotion, approached the couple. "Love in the face of death," he mused aloud, his voice dripping with sarcasm. "How touching."

Elsie, her voice filled with a mixture of fear and defiance, spoke up. "It's love that keeps us going. Even in a place like this."

Heinz leaned down, his face inches from Elsie's. "Then let's test that theory, shall we?" he whispered, a malicious glint in his eyes.

He ordered the guards to separate them. Karl, barely conscious, was dragged to the infirmary, while Elsie was taken to a solitary confinement cell.

Locked away in the cold, dark cell, every minute felt like an eternity for Elsie. The only solace she had was the memory of that brief moment with Karl, the warmth of their embrace amidst the chilling cold of Auschwitz.

In the infirmary, Karl slowly regained consciousness, the face of Elsie haunting his every thought. He was determined to see her again, to ensure her safety amidst the dangers of the camp.

Days turned into nights and nights into days, with both Elsie and Karl enduring their own forms of torment. But their love, tested by the fires of Auschwitz and the cruelty of Oberst Heinz, remained unbroken.

Elsie, sat in her cell, humming a tune they had once shared—a beacon of hope, a promise of reunion, a defiance against the hell on earth they found themselves in.

5

A GLIMMER OF HOPE

The days in Auschwitz were long, the nights even longer, and time seemed to stretch in a painful, monotonous loop. The gruelling routine had taken a toll on Elsie, leaving her a shadow of her former self. Her once-vibrant eyes now reflected the sorrow and despair that surrounded her. The music, the art, the very essence of her being, seemed like a distant dream in this hellish reality.

One bitterly cold morning, as the prisoners were being herded out of their barracks for the day's labour, Elsie stumbled, her weakened state making it difficult to keep pace with the rest. A guard, notorious for his cruelty, saw this as an opportunity to exert his power. With a malicious grin, he approached her, raising his whip menacingly.

As the leather strip descended towards Elsie, an unexpected intervention occurred. A fellow prisoner, wearing the striped uniform stained with grime and sweat, stepped in front, taking the brunt of the lash across his back. He crumpled in pain but managed to shield Elsie from further harm.

Elsie, dazed and still reeling from the near assault, tried to thank her saviour, but the man, his face shadowed by a tattered cap, simply nodded and whispered, "Stay strong." Without another word, he disappeared into the throng of prisoners.

Though their interaction was brief, the man's act of bravery and selflessness left a lasting impression on Elsie. She yearned to find him, to properly express her gratitude, but the vastness of the camp and the grim routine made it nearly impossible.

Unbeknownst to Elsie, her saviour was none other than Karl. The harrowing conditions of the camp, coupled with the weight of despair and constant fear, had aged him. His once-steady eyes now held the weight of unspoken traumas, and his physique, once sturdy, was gaunt from malnutrition and toil.

Karl, for his part, hadn't recognized Elsie either. The woman he had protected seemed far from the vibrant, passionate artist he had fallen in love with. However, something deep within, a subconscious pull, had driven him to act on her behalf.

As the days passed, Elsie became more determined to find the stranger who had shown her kindness. She began to ask around discreetly, describing the incident and hoping someone might know the man's identity. Whispers of the act of bravery had spread through the camp, and many pointed her towards Karl, describing him as a quiet, resilient prisoner who often stood up against the guards' cruelty.

One evening, as the sun cast long shadows across the camp, Elsie found herself near the men's barracks, drawn by the soft strains of a harmonica. The tune was melancholic but filled with a sense of hope. Following the music, she arrived at a small gathering of prisoners, where in the centre, playing the instrument, was the man who had saved her.

Karl, lost in the music, didn't initially notice Elsie's approach. But as the final notes faded and the small applause from the surrounding prisoners filled the air, their eyes met. Recognition didn't dawn immediately. Instead, there was a shared moment of gratitude and understanding.

Elsie stepped forward, her voice quivering, "I've been searching for you. You saved me."

Karl, looking deeply into her eyes, replied, "I did what anyone would've done."

As they conversed, the familiarity of their connection began to resurface. They spoke of their past, their dreams, their hopes, and the cruel twist of fate that had brought them to Auschwitz. It was only when Elsie mentioned her sketches and her love for music did Karl's memory jolt.

"Elsie?" he whispered, his eyes widening in realization.

Tears streamed down Elsie's face as she nodded, "Karl?"

In the midst of hell on earth, amidst the pain and despair, their reunion was a glimmer of hope, a testament to the endurance of the human spirit and the bonds of love.

They clung to each other, finding solace in their shared pain and memories. The horrors of the camp seemed momentarily distant, replaced by the warmth of their embrace.

Word of their reunion spread throughout the camp, and for many, it became a symbol of hope. If love could endure the harshest of conditions, then perhaps there was hope for a brighter tomorrow.

They sat in silence, drawing strength from each other's presence, the cool night air making them shiver slightly. The camp, with its watchtowers and electrified fences, seemed eerily quiet in the nighttime, the occasional bark of a guard dog or a distant shout the only reminder of their grim reality.

Karl began to hum softly, the same tune he had played on the harmonica earlier. Elsie, recognizing it, joined in, her voice a gentle whisper in the night. The melody was a lullaby from their homeland, a tune both had heard in their childhood, a reminder of simpler times.

As they sang, other prisoners, drawn by the soft strains of the music, began to gather around. Soon, a chorus of voices rose in the night, each one singing for lost loved ones, for dreams deferred, and for a hopeful tomorrow. It was a moment of unity, of shared pain and collective hope.

In the shadows, even some guards paused to listen, the haunting melody reminding them of their own humanity, a stark contrast to the cruelty they were often tasked to inflict.

When the song ended, the night seemed a little less cold, the stars a bit brighter. Elsie leaned into Karl, resting her head on his shoulder. "Thank you," she whispered, her voice filled with emotion. "For everything."

Karl simply tightened his grip on her hand, their intertwined fingers a symbol of their unbreakable bond. "Always," he replied, echoing the promise they had made to each other.

The two of them, surrounded by fellow prisoners, looked up at the vast expanse of the sky. For that brief moment, the confines of Auschwitz melted away, replaced by dreams of freedom and a future together.

As the first rays of sunlight pierced the horizon, Elsie and Karl, hand in hand, faced a new day, their spirits buoyed by the knowledge that even in the darkest of times, love and hope could thrive.

6

OBERST'S OBSESSION

The days following Karl and Elsie's reunion were bittersweet. The joy of finding each other was tempered by the reality of their surroundings and the constant threat of Oberst Heinz's unpredictable cruelty. It became apparent to many in the camp that Karl, for reasons unknown, had drawn the particular ire of the camp commandant.

It began with small things. Karl was frequently chosen for the hardest labour details, made to work longer hours without breaks, or assigned to the most hazardous tasks. One evening, after a particularly gruelling shift, he was singled out during roll call and subjected to a public beating, the guards taking turns to strike him while Oberst Heinz watched with a cold, sadistic pleasure.

News of this incident reached Elsie, filling her with dread and helplessness. She began to use her position in the infirmary to gather supplies and medicine, secreting away bandages and pain relievers whenever she could.

One evening, as Karl was being escorted back to his barracks after another round of torture, he collapsed from exhaustion and pain. Instead of being left to die, he was, surprisingly, taken to the infirmary. Perhaps Oberst Heinz found more satisfaction in seeing Karl suffer for longer, or perhaps there were other motivations at play.

Elsie, upon seeing Karl's battered and bruised form, felt a surge of emotion—rage, despair, but most of all, a fierce determination to protect him. She tended to his wounds, her touch gentle, whispering words of comfort and hope.

"Why is he doing this?" she whispered, more to herself than Karl.

Karl, through cracked lips and with great effort, replied, "He sees me as a challenge, someone to break. Every time he tries to crush my spirit and I rise again, it only fuels his obsession."

Elsie, tears streaming down her face, vowed, "We will get through this, together."

Over the following days, Elsie became Karl's shadow, using every opportunity to care for him, to shield him from further harm. She began to trade her meagre rations and personal belongings with other prisoners in exchange for information or Favors that might protect Karl.

She even tried to approach the older prison guard who had shown her kindness before, hoping to appeal to his humanity. The guard, while sympathetic, warned her of the dangers of drawing too much attention. "Oberst Heinz is a man consumed by his demons," he murmured. "Be careful."

However, as days turned into weeks, Oberst Heinz's obsession with Karl only intensified. It seemed as though he had made it his personal mission to break Karl's spirit. He would taunt him, subjecting him to physical and psychological torments, always watching for any sign of surrender.

One particularly chilling evening, Oberst Heinz summoned Karl to his personal quarters. The room was stark, filled with military paraphernalia, and cold, much like Heinz himself. He offered Karl a seat and poured him a glass of schnapps.

"This can all end, you know," Heinz began, swirling the liquid in his glass. "All you have to do is submit. Admit defeat."

Karl, though weakened and in pain, met Heinz's gaze evenly. "I may be imprisoned, but my spirit remains free. You can never take that away."

Heinz's face darkened. "We shall see," he hissed.

Karl was taken immediately to the confinement block by guards. The corridor inside was dimly lit, the air thick with a mix of dampness and the lingering stench of despair. It was lined with doors, behind each of which lay tiny cells meant for solitary confinement. The guards roughly pushed Karl into one of these cells and slammed the door shut.

The cell was a grim testament to the camp's cruelty. Barely five feet in length and width, it was a claustrophobic box of cold, rough-hewn stone. The ceiling, oppressively low, added to the cell's suffocating nature. There was no window, just a tiny vent near the ceiling, too high to reach, ensuring that the room was perpetually shrouded in semi-darkness. The only furniture was a thin wooden plank that served as a bed, without any bedding or cushioning.

The silence within the cell was deafening. The thick walls muffled the outside world's sounds, leaving Karl trapped with his thoughts. Time seemed to warp, with minutes feeling like hours and hours like days. The lack of stimuli, the pressing solitude, and the darkness threatened to break his spirit.

Food, when it was provided, was pushed through a small gap at the bottom of the door. It was even more meagre than the camp's already paltry rations, often just a crust of bread and some water. Karl had to grope in the dark to find his sustenance, each morsel reminding him of his grim situation.

The physical discomfort of the confinement— the cold, the hunger, the aching stiffness from the cramped space— was harrowing. But it was the psychological torment that proved even more challenging. The isolation gnawed at Karl's mind, causing him to relive his worst memories, amplifying his fears and anxieties.

Every so often, the door's heavy bolt would scrape, signalling the entrance of a guard. More often than not, it was to deliver a beating, a cruel reminder of Heinz's power. Bruised and battered, Karl would then be left alone once more, the echoes of the guard's departing laughter a cruel accompaniment to his solitude.

In that dim, confined space, Karl found strength in memories of Elsie. He would recall their shared moments, their dreams, and their unwavering love for one another. These memories became his lifeline, a beacon of hope in his windowless abyss.

Days turned into weeks. The passage of time was marked only by the gradual weakening of his body and the constant churn of his mind. But throughout his ordeal in solitary confinement, Karl's spirit, though tested, remained unbroken, a silent testament to human resilience in the face of overwhelming adversity.

Elsie, desperate and terrified for Karl's well-being, hatched a risky plan. Using her connections in the infirmary and with the help of a few trusted prisoners, she managed to smuggle in small notes to Karl, each filled with words of love and encouragement. These tiny pieces of paper, filled with hope and affection, became Karl's lifeline, a beacon in his darkest hours.

Elsie, having gathered enough evidence of Heinz's cruelties, decided to approach some of the senior officers in the camp, hoping to appeal to their sense of duty or perhaps leverage any underlying rivalries.

Cornering Heinz in his office, her voice shaking but determined, Elsie declared, "Your obsession with Karl ends now. If not, your superiors will hear of your... indiscretions."

Heinz, for the first time, looked taken aback. But his surprise quickly turned to rage. "You're playing a dangerous game," he growled.

Elsie, summoning all her courage, replied, "A game you started. Now it's time for it to end."

The tension in the room was palpable, a battle of wills between two individuals, one fighting for love, the other for control. The room was thick with anticipation, each person awaiting the other's move.

After what felt like an eternity, Heinz broke the silence, his voice dripping with menace. "You're brave, I'll give you that. But bravery can be...misguided."

Elsie, her heart pounding but her gaze unwavering, countered, "What's misguided is thinking you can break the human spirit with cruelty and obsession. Karl is stronger than you think, and so am I."

Heinz leaned in, his face inches from Elsie's. "You're playing with fire. If you push too hard, you might not like the consequences."

Elsie took a deep breath, drawing upon every ounce of strength she possessed. "Then let the flames rise. Because I will do whatever it takes to protect those I love."

The two stared each other down, the tension palpable. But after a long moment, Heinz leaned back, a sardonic smile playing on his lips. "Very well," he said coldly. "But remember this: the game has changed, and I always play to win."

He signalled for the guards to escort Elsie out. As she walked away, she could feel Heinz's piercing gaze on her, but she held her head high, determination burning in her heart.

News of Elsie's confrontation with Heinz spread throughout the camp, and she became something of a legend among the prisoners. Her courage in standing up to the fearsome commandant gave many a renewed sense of hope and strength.

However, the repercussions of her actions were felt quickly. While Heinz did reduce his direct torments on Karl, he tightened his grip on the camp, becoming even more unpredictable and brutal. The atmosphere grew even more oppressive, with everyone on edge, wondering when Heinz's next cruel whim would strike.

Elsie's confrontation with Oberst Heinz, though borne out of a desperate need to protect Karl, had far-reaching consequences that rippled through the camp with a chilling effect. In the wake of their encounter, a silent yet palpable shift occurred. Heinz, his ego bruised by Elsie's audacity, sought to reassert his control over Auschwitz with renewed ferocity.

The camp, already a place of despair, became further steeped in fear. Heinz's actions grew more erratic and punitive. The prisoners whispered among themselves that the commandant had become like a wounded animal, lashing out in unpredictable ways. Roll calls became longer and more frequent, often dragging on for hours in the biting cold or blistering heat as Heinz scrutinized each prisoner with a hawk-like gaze, searching for any semblance of defiance to crush.

The meager rations, already insufficient, were cut even further on a whim. Prisoners stumbled through their forced labor weakened by hunger, the gnawing emptiness in their stomachs a constant reminder of Heinz's tightening control. The slightest misstep, an accidental drop of a tool, or a moment's rest, was met with disproportionate brutality. The guards, emboldened by Heinz's example, became more vicious, their batons and boots finding new victims daily.

Within the barracks, the air was thick with tension and mistrust. The inmates slept with one eye open, fearful that the person beside them might be driven to betrayal by desperation or Heinz's manipulations. The solidarity that once gave them strength was fraying at the edges, strained by the commandant's systematic campaign of terror.

Elsie, who had once brought a measure of hope to Karl and others, now moved through the camp with a heavy heart. Her defiance had saved Karl from Heinz's immediate wrath, but at what cost? She watched as friends and strangers alike suffered, and though she knew it was Heinz who was to blame, she couldn't help but feel the weight of their suffering as her burden to bear.

The commandant's presence hung over the camp like a dark cloud. He no longer needed to be physically present to instill fear; his very name was enough to silence conversation and quicken pulses. The cruelty of his regime was not just in the overt acts of violence, but in the psychological shadow that he cast over every corner of Auschwitz.

Even the act of escape became more daunting. The electrified fences seemed to hum with a more sinister energy, and the guards patrolled with a keener sense of purpose. The rumors of Heinz's cruelty spread beyond the confines of the camp, reaching the ears of the outside world, yet inside, the prisoners felt more isolated than ever.

In this atmosphere of heightened oppression, the prisoners were pushed to the brink. Yet, even as the darkness deepened, so too did their resolve. Amidst the suffering, small acts of resistance continued, sparks of defiance that refused to be extinguished. Elsie, Karl, and their fellow inmates clung to the hope that Heinz's reign of terror would not last forever, that justice would eventually be served, and that humanity would prevail.

Elsie and Karl, during their stolen moments together, spoke of escape, of finding a way out of the hellish landscape of Auschwitz. Their love, tested and forged in the crucible of adversity, became their guiding light, pushing them to find a way to break free from Oberst Heinz's malevolent grasp.

Elsie, Karl, and a small group of trusted inmates, huddled in the shadows, began to hatch a plan, determined to find freedom and bring an end to Heinz's reign of terror. The path ahead was uncertain and fraught with danger, but the fire of resistance, fuelled by love and hope, was burning brighter than ever.

7

LOST LETTERS

The camp's infirmary, where Elsie spent most of her days, was a place of both despair and resilience. Amidst the grim atmosphere, moments of humanity occasionally broke through the stifling weight of the camp's oppression. While treating ailing inmates, Elsie would sometimes stumble across personal belongings—photos, trinkets, and sometimes, letters. Each of these items told a silent story, a whisper from a world left behind.

One day, while cleaning a makeshift shelf, Elsie stumbled upon a bundle of letters, neatly tied with a fraying string. The topmost envelope was addressed simply to "Elsie." A pang of longing struck her heart, and she couldn't resist the urge to read them, thinking they might be the unsent words Karl had wanted to convey to her.

The letters, penned with a delicate hand and careful wording, painted a picture of a life outside the confines of the camp—a world filled with music, laughter, and love. They spoke of shared moments, stolen glances, and dreams of a future together. Each sentence conveyed a depth of emotion that resonated deeply with Elsie.

But as she continued to read, something felt amiss. References to events she didn't recognize, mentions of places she'd never been to, and, most importantly, a shared secret—a song only they knew. This wasn't their song.

With a sinking feeling, Elsie came to the painful realization that these letters, though addressed to an "Elsie," weren't meant for her. The woman Karl was writing to, the one he shared these intimate moments with, was someone else from his past.

The weight of this revelation sat heavy in Elsie's heart. Questions swirled in her mind. Who was this other Elsie? What had she meant to Karl? And why had he never spoken of her?

Days passed, and the knowledge of the letters ate away at Elsie. She wanted to confront Karl, to seek clarity, but fear held her back—fear of what the truth might reveal, fear of what it might do to their relationship.

One evening, as the camp settled into its restless sleep, Elsie approached Karl's barracks, the bundle of letters clutched tightly in her hand. Finding a quiet corner, she mustered the courage to speak.

"These are yours," she began, her voice shaky, handing him the letters.

Karl looked at the bundle, recognition and surprise evident in his eyes. "Where did you find these?" he asked, taking them gently.

"In the infirmary," she replied, her voice barely above a whisper. "I read them, Karl."

A heavy silence settled between them. Karl took a deep breath, his eyes filled with a mixture of sorrow and regret. "Elsie," he began, choosing his words carefully, "before the war, before all of this, there was someone in my life. Another Elsie."

He went on to explain how they had met in Berlin, both young and full of dreams. They shared a love for music, art, and literature, losing themselves in the city's vibrant culture. But as the political climate changed and the Nazis rose to power, their world began to crumble. The last he heard, she had fled to Switzerland, hoping to find refuge there. He had written these letters over the years, holding onto the hope that he would someday find her and give them to her.

Elsie, tears streaming down her face, listened intently. The pain of the revelation was sharp, but hearing Karl's earnest words, she felt a deep sense of understanding. "Why didn't you tell me?" she asked, her voice filled with hurt.

Karl, reaching out to hold her hand, replied, "I didn't want our love to be overshadowed by the past. What we have, here and now, is real. I didn't want to burden you with my old sorrows."

The two sat together, the weight of their shared pain and understanding binding them closer. The past, with its joys and sorrows, was a part of them, but it did not define their present.

Elsie and Karl, sitting under the vast expanse of the night sky, finding solace in their shared moments. The letters, though a painful revelation, became a testament to their resilience and the understanding that love, in all its forms, has the power to heal and bind.

Elsie, her emotions in turmoil, took a moment to process everything. "Karl," she began, her voice quivering, "in a place like this, where every moment could be our last, honesty means everything."

Karl nodded, his eyes downcast. "You're right. I should've told you sooner."

The two sat in silence, the weight of the revelation hanging between them. But as the minutes ticked by, a newfound understanding began to take shape. Elsie realized that the past was just that—the past. And while it was a part of Karl's journey, it didn't diminish the love and connection they shared in the present.

"You loved her," Elsie murmured, not as an accusation, but as a simple acknowledgment.

Karl looked up, his eyes filled with a mix of pain and nostalgia. "I did. But that was another life, another time. Here, with you, I've found a love that's helped me endure the unimaginable. And for that, I'll be forever grateful."

Elsie, drawing strength from his words, gently placed a hand on his cheek. "Love is complicated," she whispered. "But here, in this place, it's also our salvation. We must hold onto it, no matter what."

The two leaned into each other, finding solace in their shared embrace. Around them, the camp, with its ever-present dangers and sorrow, seemed to fade away, if only for a brief moment.

In the days that followed, the bond between Elsie and Karl grew stronger. They began to share more of their past, opening up about the joys, sorrows, and dreams they once held. It was a way of reclaiming their humanity, of reminding themselves that they were more than just prisoners, more than just numbers.

The letters, once a source of pain, became a bridge to understanding. Karl would read them aloud to Elsie, sharing stories of his past, of the other Elsie, and of a Berlin that once was. And in return, Elsie would share her own memories, painting a vivid picture of her life before the war.

The two are sat together, the bundle of letters beside them. But instead of looking to the past, they're making plans for the future, dreaming of a world beyond the barbed wires, where love and hope can truly flourish.

8

UNSPOKEN BOND

In the subsequent weeks, Auschwitz bore witness to the blossoming bond between Karl and Elsie. The shadows of their past had been cast away, allowing their relationship to flourish in the stark reality of the present. Amidst the heart-wrenching cries and torments of the camp, their shared moments became an oasis of peace, a sanctuary where love could dare to exist.

Each day, after their respective gruelling tasks, they'd meet at a secluded spot near the barbed wires—a place where, if you squinted just right, the menacing fences seemed to disappear, replaced by the vast expanse of the sky. Here, they'd share stories, laugh, dream, and more often than not, find solace in each other's silent company.

Karl often brought his harmonica, its melancholic tunes blending seamlessly with the evening's cool breeze. Elsie, with her knowledge of art, would describe paintings in vivid detail, transporting them both to grand galleries far from the prison's confines. These moments, simple yet profound, forged an unbreakable connection between the two.

One evening, as the sun painted the sky with hues of gold and crimson, Elsie turned to Karl, her eyes searching his. "Do you ever wonder," she began hesitantly, "if our paths might've crossed before all this? If fate had intertwined our destinies even before we met here?"

Karl pondered the question, his fingers absentmindedly playing a soft tune on the harmonica. "Perhaps," he replied thoughtfully, "but does it really matter? I believe that every moment, every encounter, has its own significance. Our bond, Elsie, is born out of our shared experiences here, out of our resilience and hope. And that's more powerful than any past connection could ever be."

Elsie smiled, her heart warmed by his words. "You're right," she whispered, leaning her head on his shoulder. "It's the present that matters. It's the love we've found amidst this chaos."

Days turned into weeks, and their routine continued. Word of their bond spread throughout the camp, and for many, their relationship became a symbol of hope. It was a testament to the indomitable human spirit, proof that love could thrive even in the darkest of times.

However, the world outside their haven was unpredictable. Oberst Heinz's erratic behaviour and the ever-looming threat of separation kept them on edge. But they had made a silent pact—to cherish every moment and to face challenges head-on, together.

One day, a rumour began circulating that a group of prisoners would be transferred to another camp. The anxiety was palpable. Families and loved ones clung to each other, praying they wouldn't be torn apart. Elsie and Karl, knowing the unpredictability of their situation, held each other tighter.

That night, as they met at their usual spot, Karl had a surprise for Elsie. He had crafted a small pendant from bits of scrap metal, fashioned into a heart. "I wanted you to have something," he said, his voice choked with emotion, "a reminder of our time together, no matter where we end up."

Elsie, tears glistening in her eyes, clutched the pendant to her chest. "Karl," she whispered, "this means everything. Just like you."

The evening was filled with a bittersweet mix of emotions—love, fear, and an unwavering determination to stay together.

Elsie and Karl sat gazing at the stars, their fingers entwined. Words were no longer necessary. Their bond, forged in the crucible of Auschwitz, spoke volumes. The future was uncertain, but their love, rooted firmly in the present, was a beacon of hope, guiding them through the darkest nights.

In the days that followed, the atmosphere in the camp grew tenser. Whispers of the upcoming transfer intensified, with everyone fearing the worst. Yet, amidst this backdrop of uncertainty, Karl and Elsie's bond seemed to defy the very reality they were ensnared in.

Their secluded spot by the fences became a refuge not just for them, but for others too. Word spread about the couple who had found love in the most unlikely of places, and soon, others began to join them in the evenings. Some would bring instruments, some would share stories, and others would simply sit in silent contemplation, drawing strength from the collective spirit of hope.

One evening, a frail old man approached them. He introduced himself as Rabbi Weiss. With tears in his eyes, he spoke of his lost family and how the tales of Karl and Elsie's love had given him a reason to go on. He shared verses from scriptures, speaking of undying love and the power of the human spirit. The three sat, their souls intertwined in shared grief and newfound hope.

The night before the rumoured transfers, the camp was eerily silent, the usual sounds of anguish replaced by a heavy stillness. Karl and Elsie met, their hearts heavy with unspoken fears.

Elsie, clutching the pendant Karl had given her, whispered, "Promise me something."

"Anything," Karl replied, his gaze locked onto hers.

"If we get separated," she began, her voice breaking, "promise me that you'll remember our time here, that you'll hold onto our love and let it guide you."

Karl, taking her hand, pressed it to his lips. "Always," he vowed. "No matter where we are, our souls are forever entwined."

As dawn broke, the camp was awakened by the shrill whistle of the guards. The dreaded day had come. Prisoners were herded like cattle, lists were read out, and families and loved ones clung to each other in desperate farewell.

Karl and Elsie, their hands tightly clasped, awaited their fate. But fate, as always, was unpredictable. Elsie's name was called, but Karl's wasn't. As she was pulled away, their fingers desperately tried to hold onto each other, their eyes conveying a depth of emotion words could never capture.

Elsie was pushed into a truck, her eyes locked onto Karl's till the very last moment. But even in this painful goodbye, their love remained unwavering, an unspoken bond that would always tether their souls together, no matter the distance.

9

PLAN OF ESCAPE

The days following Elsie and Karl's separation were agony for both of them. Elsie, transported to a separate block, was constantly surrounded by unfamiliar faces. While she tried to gather information about Karl's condition, Oberst Heinz's continued obsession with him made any direct communication nearly impossible.

Rumours painted a grim picture: Karl was often dragged out for long interrogations and punishments, sometimes disappearing for days on end. The thought of him suffering at the hands of Heinz and his cronies was unbearable for Elsie. Fuelled by desperation, she began to form the kernel of a daring plan.

Late at night, in the secrecy of the barracks, she started to gather a group of trusted inmates. Each brought a unique skill to the table.

Anya was born in 1915 in Kraków, Poland, into a family of intellectuals. Her father, Aleksander, was a well-respected professor of literature at Jagiellonian University, while her mother, Zofia, was a renowned concert pianist. With two younger brothers to dote on and a home filled with books, music, and spirited debates, Anya's early years were both sheltered and intellectually stimulating.

However, this idyllic world began to shift when Anya was in her twenties. The rise of anti-Semitism, even before the Nazi invasion, became increasingly palpable in her beloved Kraków. Her family faced social isolation, and there were murmurs about her father losing his professorship because of his Jewish heritage.

In these challenging times, Anya found solace in her close-knit group of friends, young intellectuals and artists who often met at the city's cafes. Here, amidst whispered conversations and hushed poetry readings, the seeds of resistance were sown. Anya, with her fiery spirit and razor-sharp intellect, quickly became a key figure within this group.

When the Nazis invaded Poland in 1939, the situation went from bad to worse. The Jews of Kraków were subjected to escalating persecution. Anya's family, like many others, was forcibly relocated to the Kraków Ghetto. It was here that Anya's role in the resistance solidified. Drawing on her network of friends and acquaintances, she played a pivotal role in establishing underground communication channels, smuggling food, medicine, and, most crucially, information.

Tragically, in a raid on the ghetto, Anya's parents and one of her brothers were rounded up and deported, their fates unknown but feared. This personal loss only fuelled Anya's resolve to fight the Nazi regime.

Joining forces with the Polish underground, Anya's home soon became a hub for covert operations. She was instrumental in saving dozens of Jewish children, smuggling them out of the ghetto to safe houses or sympathetic Polish families willing to hide them.

Her daring exploits earned her a reputation, and she became known as "The Flame" within resistance circles - a beacon of hope in those dark times.

However, her activities did not go unnoticed. In 1942, following a tip-off, the Gestapo raided her hideout. While she managed to escape the dragnet, she was on the run. Moving from one safe house to another, she continued her resistance activities until she was eventually captured during a raid in late 1943.

Sent to Auschwitz, Anya's reputation preceded her. But even within the camp's brutal confines, she refused to be silenced, forming covert support groups, organizing secret educational sessions, and even planning escapes.

Markus Steinberg, born in 1907 in Leipzig, Germany, was the embodiment of perseverance. His father, Wilhelm, ran a small but thriving watchmaking business, while his mother, Clara, dedicated her life to her children and community work. Markus grew up alongside two sisters in a neighbourhood where the echoes of children's laughter mingled with the rhythmic sounds of his father's workshop.

From a young age, Markus displayed a keen interest in mechanics. Hours turned into days as he sat with his father, learning the intricate art of watchmaking. By his late teens, Markus had not only mastered the trade but introduced innovative techniques that significantly improved the efficiency of the family business.

But as the 1930s progressed, the growing tide of anti-Semitism began to impact the Steinberg family. Their loyal clientele dwindled, replaced by hostile glares and whispered threats. Yet, Markus, with his broad frame and imposing presence, often served as a protective barrier between the escalating external hatred and his family. He earned the nickname "The Silent Guardian" among locals, always watching, always ready to shield his loved ones from harm.

When the Nuremberg Laws were enacted in 1935, the Steinberg watchmaking business was seized. Heartbroken but undeterred, Markus relocated his family to a smaller apartment and took up clandestine jobs repairing timepieces, all the while ensuring his younger sisters continued their education.

With the intensification of Nazi persecution, Markus joined an underground resistance group, assisting in smuggling Jewish families to neighbouring countries. His mechanical prowess proved invaluable, as he rigged hidden compartments in vehicles and developed coded communication tools for the group.

However, in 1941, during a covert operation, Markus was captured. Despite enduring brutal interrogations, he never revealed any information about his comrades. His resilience landed him in Auschwitz, where his formidable stature caught the eye of the guards. They assigned him to gruelling manual labour, believing the backbreaking work would quickly break him.

In Auschwitz, Markus's path intertwined with Karl and Elsie. Recognizing the threat posed by Oberst Heinz to Karl, Markus often stepped in subtly, using his imposing presence as a deterrent and silently signalling to Karl to tread carefully.

Though a man of few words, Markus's actions spoke volumes. In the camp's brutal environment, he became a beacon of hope and strength, embodying the belief that even in the face of overwhelming darkness, the human spirit's resilience could shine through.

Joseph Müller, born in the heart of Berlin in 1898, grew up in a city alive with culture, innovation, and ambition. From a young age, he displayed an uncanny knack for observation. By the age of 10, he could recount minute details others overlooked, making him the undisputed champion of family games and the occasional neighbourhood mystery.

His parents, both of whom were teachers, instilled in him a deep respect for justice and integrity. Drawing inspiration from his childhood heroes—fictional detectives from the novels he devoured—Joseph decided to pursue a career in law enforcement.

By his mid-twenties, he had ascended the ranks to become a detective in the Berlin Police Department. His unparalleled observation skills, combined with a sharp analytical mind, led him to crack some of the city's most perplexing cases. But beyond the accolades and respect, Joseph was driven by a profound sense of duty. To him, every solved case meant justice for a victim and peace for a family.

However, as the 1930s unfolded and the Nazis took power, Joseph's position became increasingly untenable. The ideals he held dear—justice, truth, integrity—were being systematically eroded. He watched with growing dismay as many of his colleagues became instruments of the Nazi regime, turning a blind eye to atrocities or, worse, participating in them.

Joseph's breaking point came when he was ordered to lead investigations against Jewish business owners based on fabricated evidence. Torn between his duty as a detective and his moral compass, he made a courageous choice: he discreetly sabotaged these investigations, ensuring that they led to dead ends.

Word of his covert defiance inevitably reached his superiors. Though he evaded immediate capture thanks to inside information from a sympathetic colleague, Joseph knew his days in Berlin were numbered. He went underground, using his investigative skills to aid the fledgling resistance movement. He became an expert in forging documents, helping countless Jews and political dissidents escape the Nazi dragnet.

But in 1942, a sting operation went awry, and Joseph was captured and sent to Auschwitz. The Nazis were aware of his skills, and he was often forced to participate in cruel interrogations, always walking a tightrope between assisting his captors and subtly sabotaging their efforts.

In Auschwitz, Joseph's path converged with those of Elsie, Karl, Markus, and Anya. Together, they formed an unlikely alliance—a bond forged in the fires of adversity. Through whispers and coded messages, Joseph became a vital conduit for information, always strategizing, always one step ahead, proving that even in the darkest corners, the detective's sharp mind was his greatest weapon.

Together, under the cover of darkness, they began plotting. The plan was simple yet audacious: They would create a diversion, overpower the guards during the ensuing chaos, and smuggle Karl out through a series of underground tunnels that some inmates had been secretly digging for months.

The key to the plan's success lay in its timing. They needed a moment when the guards would be least vigilant and most susceptible to distraction. Markus suggested targeting the weekly shipments that came into the camp. The guards, often busy with unloading and revelling in their newly acquired contraband, would be momentarily distracted.

Elsie, drawing on her knowledge of Oberst Heinz's routines, proposed adding a personal touch to the diversion. "Heinz has a certain... ritual," she explained. "Every Wednesday evening, he enjoys a bottle of schnapps from the latest shipment, usually in his office. If we could tamper with that bottle..."

Joseph interjected, "A sedative? Something to make him unconscious or at least, severely incapacitated?"

Anya nodded, "I've heard whispers of a doctor here, sympathetic to our cause. He might have something potent enough."

10

FATEFUL NIGHT

The night was overcast, a blanket of clouds obscuring the moon, casting Auschwitz into an even deeper gloom. Inside the camp, the atmosphere was electric, a thick tension hanging in the air, palpable and foreboding. Elsie, Karl, and their band of trusted inmates knew that tonight was the night their meticulously planned escape would be set in motion. It was a gamble of the highest stakes, but in their hearts, they understood that the alternative was even bleaker.

Elsie, her pulse quickening, reviewed the plan one last time with the group. Markus had managed to fashion a rudimentary tool, sharpened and capable of cutting through the fence. Anya had sourced a small batch of homemade explosives, intended to create a diversion and draw the guards away from their escape route. Joseph, using his detective insights, had mapped out the weakest points of the camp's security. Everything was in place.

Yet, as the minutes ticked away, an undeniable fear gnawed at Elsie's heart. The image of Karl, battered and weakened from his encounters with Oberst Heinz, weighed heavily on her mind. She shook off the creeping dread, steeling herself for the task at hand. They had one shot at this, and failure wasn't an option.

As the clock's hands neared midnight, Anya took her position near the main watchtower. With a swift and practiced motion, she lit the fuse of the explosive. The ensuing blast sent shockwaves throughout the camp. Flames licked the night sky, casting eerie, dancing shadows on the ground. As anticipated, the guards, disoriented and panicking, rushed towards the source of the explosion.

Seizing this golden window of opportunity, Elsie, Karl, Markus, and a handful of other inmates dashed towards the camp's eastern fence, the furthest point from the explosion. Markus, with sweat dripping from his brow, worked furiously to cut through the imposing barrier. Each second felt like an eternity, the distant shouts and chaos serving as a grim reminder of the danger they were in.

Finally, with a triumphant whisper, Markus managed to create an opening just wide enough for them to slip through. One by one, they crawled to freedom, their hearts pounding in their chests.

However, as the last of the escapees made their way out, a blinding searchlight illuminated the fence, and the sharp crack of a gunshot echoed through the night. Joseph, who was covering their exit, was hit. He crumpled to the ground, blood seeping into the cold earth beneath him.

Elsie, horror gripping her, rushed to his side. But Joseph, with his dying breaths, urged her on. "Go," he rasped, his voice weak but resolute. "Promise me you'll find freedom."

Tears streaming down her face, Elsie nodded, clutching his hand. "I promise," she whispered, pressing a gentle kiss to his forehead.

With a renewed sense of urgency, the group plunged into the dense forest that bordered the camp. The canopy above swallowed them, the trees providing a temporary shield from their pursuers. They navigated through the treacherous terrain, guided only by the North Star.

As dawn began to break, Elsie, Karl, and the remaining escapees found themselves at the edge of a clearing. Exhausted, both physically and emotionally, they decided to rest, taking turns to keep watch.

Karl, his face etched with fatigue and worry, pulled Elsie close. "We made it," he murmured, his voice choked with emotion.

Elsie, her eyes red-rimmed from tears, nodded. "Yes, but at such a cost."

They both thought of Joseph, his sacrifice ensuring their escape. In the stillness of the morning, amidst the chorus of birdsong, they took a moment to honour him and the countless others who had paid the ultimate price for freedom.

The group, rejuvenated by a brief respite, prepare to continue their journey. The path to safety was still long and fraught with peril, but they had taken the first, crucial step. And with each passing moment, the horrors of Auschwitz receded further into the distance, replaced by the promise of a new beginning.

In the dappled light of the early morning, the survivors huddled together, drawing warmth and strength from their shared experience. A makeshift fire crackled in the centre, the flames' dance casting fleeting, golden patterns on the faces that encircled it.

Karl, with a distant look in his eyes, reached into his pocket, retrieving the harmonica he had clung to throughout their ordeal. Placing it to his lips, he played a haunting melody, a tune of sorrow, of memories lost but not forgotten. The notes, so raw and powerful, seemed to capture the very essence of their journey.

Elsie listened, tears streaming unabated, the music transporting her back to moments in the camp – their first meeting, the whispered dreams, the stolen glances. Every note resonated deeply, etching itself onto her soul.

Anya, her usually fiery spirit subdued, joined in with a soft lullaby, her voice blending seamlessly with Karl's melody. The combined effect was mesmerizing, a symphony of pain, hope, and resilience.

As the song reached its crescendo, a piercing cry echoed in the distance—a warning. The Nazis were closing in.

Instantly, the group was on high alert. The fire was doused, and every trace of their brief rest was erased. With Markus leading the way, they plunged deeper into the forest, their every sense attuned to the dangers around them.

Hours seemed to merge, the dense foliage and rugged terrain making their journey treacherous. But every step took them further from Auschwitz and the nightmares it held.

Late in the afternoon, they stumbled upon a hidden cave, its entrance obscured by thick undergrowth. Deciding it was a suitable place to rest and regroup, they ventured inside. The cave was surprisingly spacious, it's cool interior offering a welcome respite.

Using the brief pause to their advantage, they discussed their next move. They needed to reach a safe point, a location where the resistance could shelter them. Anya, with contacts in the underground network, mentioned a safe house located in a village not too far from their current location.

Determined, the group set this as their next destination. The journey would be perilous, but the promise of safety and sanctuary drove them forward.

The night was spent in tense vigilance, with Elsie and Karl taking a moment to share a quiet conversation.

"Do you think we'll ever find peace, Elsie?" Karl whispered, his voice heavy with emotion.

Elsie, gazing deep into his eyes, replied, "We already have, in a way. In our bond, in our love. The world outside might be chaotic, but as long as we have each other, we have a piece of peace."

Their tender moment was interrupted by the first light of dawn, signalling the beginning of another day on the run. The group packed up and began their trek towards the safe house.

As the cave fades into the distance, the silhouette of the group moving forward symbolized their unwavering determination. The road ahead was fraught with danger, but they were united in purpose, driven by the dream of a life free from the shadows of Auschwitz.

Hours seemed to blend into one another as they navigated the treacherous forest terrain. Just as the first rays of dawn began to pierce the horizon, Markus, using his keen sense of direction, led them to a hidden clearing. A dilapidated cabin stood in its centre, its windows boarded up, and a thin trail of smoke rising from its chimney.

The group approached cautiously, their senses on high alert. As they neared the entrance, the door creaked open to reveal a middle-aged woman, her face etched with lines of hardship but her eyes warm and welcoming.

"I've been expecting you," she said simply, ushering them inside.

The interior of the cabin was modest but cozy. The warmth from a roaring fireplace greeted them, and the tantalizing aroma of freshly baked bread filled the air. The woman introduced herself as Magda, a member of the Polish resistance.

Magda Weiss was born in 1912 in the picturesque town of Český Krumlov, nestled in the rolling hills of Bohemia. Her hometown, with its enchanting castle and winding cobblestone streets, seemed like a place where fairy tales could come to life. Her parents owned a small yet renowned pottery workshop that catered to both locals and tourists enchanted by the unique Bohemian designs.

Magda's childhood was coloured by the hues of clay and glaze. She spent countless hours in the workshop, her fingers dancing over wet clay, melding and shaping with an innate sense of artistry. By her teenage years, Magda had developed her signature style - pottery that bore the intricate patterns of Bohemian folklore, combined with a modern flair.

Despite her talents, life wasn't without challenges. Magda belonged to the small Jewish community of Český Krumlov. As the shadows of anti-Semitism lengthened across Europe, even this quaint town wasn't spared. The initial murmurs of prejudice grew louder, and the once-welcoming neighbours began to look at the Weiss family with suspicion.

In the early 1930s, smitten by a young musician named Tomas, Magda found solace in love. Their courtship was a blend of melodies and clay, music, and art. They dreamt of a future together, of combining their crafts, and perhaps even opening a cafe where people could enjoy music amidst art.

But the Nazi occupation of Czechoslovakia in 1939 crushed these dreams. Magda's workshop was seized, and her artworks were either destroyed or appropriated. Tomas, an outspoken critic of the Nazi regime, was arrested, leaving Magda heartbroken.

Refusing to succumb to despair, Magda used her artistic skills to aid the resistance. She crafted secret compartments in pottery pieces to smuggle messages and small supplies. But in 1943, a piece containing sensitive information was accidentally sold and ended up in the hands of a Gestapo officer. The discovery led to her capture.

In Auschwitz, Magda's dainty hands, which once moulded beautiful pottery, now bore the brunt of hard labour. Yet, her spirit remained unbroken. She secretly sculpted miniature figurines from scraps, a silent act of resistance and a testament to her indomitable spirit.

Magda's salvation came from an unexpected source. One evening, while she was working in one of the camp's auxiliary storage units, she overheard two guards discussing a supply transport scheduled to depart Auschwitz for a camp in Germany. The transport was rumoured to be lightly guarded due to the diversion of forces to combat the advancing Allies.

Magda, using her keen sense of observation, began to scout the area around the transport's loading zone. She noticed that large wooden crates filled with confiscated belongings were being prepared for the journey. With her experience in the family pottery workshop, Magda understood the structure and weak points of these crates.

Late one night, with the help of trusted others in the camp, Magda began her audacious plan. They carefully pried open the bottom of one of the crates, removed some of its contents, and created a hidden cavity just big enough for her to curl into. The next challenge was smuggling food and water for the journey, which one of her friends, managed to procure and discreetly place inside the crate.

The night before the transport, Magda said her heartfelt goodbyes to her friends, with each of them knowing the risks involved. She a small p was given a pendant for luck, a cherished possession she had managed to hide from the guards.

As dawn broke, Magda, concealed in her wooden sanctuary, was loaded onto the transport. The journey was harrowing. The lack of ventilation in the crate made breathing laborious, and the constant jostling threatened to give away her presence. Hours seemed like days, each minute fraught with the fear of discovery.

Upon reaching its destination, the transport was hastily unloaded. Magda, summoning all her courage, waited for nightfall before prying her way out of the crate. Using the cover of darkness and the chaos caused by air raids, she made her escape into the neighbouring woods.

In the subsequent days, Magda navigated through the German countryside, relying on her wits, the kindness of anti-Nazi sympathizers, and the guidance of the local resistance. After several close calls and countless sleepless nights, she crossed into Allied-occupied territory, finally tasting the sweet air of freedom and made her way to the cabin, which had been used by the Resistance on previous occasions.

Magda's escape from Auschwitz became a legend among the survivors, a beacon of hope in the face of insurmountable odds, and a testament to the indomitable spirit of humanity.

She had been in contact with informants within Auschwitz and had been forewarned of their escape.

The cabin, cloaked in the dense foliage of the surrounding forest, had become a haven for Elsie, Karl, and the ragtag group of escapees. Its rustic walls, which had once echoed with the simple joys of woodland solitude, now resonated with the weight of their clandestine meetings. Here, within this secluded refuge, they gathered around an old oaken table, its surface scarred with the marks of time, to hear Magda's briefing on the precarious situation unfolding beyond their sheltered enclave.

Magda, her face etched with both determination and fatigue, laid out the grim reality with the precision of a seasoned strategist. "The Nazis are combing the area with renewed vigor," she began, her voice a low whisper that demanded attention. "Oberst Heinz, that merciless commandant from Auschwitz, has been tasked with closing the net around us."

She unfurled a tattered map across the table, pointing to various locations where recent raids had intensified. "They've set up checkpoints on all major routes, and patrols are sweeping through the countryside. They're even offering rewards to locals for any information on escapees," she continued, her finger tracing the lines that represented roads now fraught with danger.

The group listened, their faces a mixture of resolve and worry. Elsie clasped Karl's hand under the table, a silent show of support as they processed the news that Heinz, the embodiment of their nightmares, was now hunting them with the desperation of a cornered predator. His brutal reputation was well known; his actions at Auschwitz had left a trail of suffering and death. The thought of falling back into his grasp was unbearable.

Magda leaned in, her eyes scanning the group. "But it's not just brute force. Heinz is cunning. He's spreading false rumors of safe passages and resistance hideouts, hoping to lure us out," she cautioned. "He's driven by a fury that we evaded his grip, and he won't stop until he's made an example of us."

The room fell into a tense silence as the weight of her words settled in their minds. The reality was clear: they were the most wanted among the escapees, not just for fleeing but for the symbolic hope their successful escape represented.

Markus, whose stoic presence had been a pillar of strength for the group, spoke up. "Then we must be smarter. We move under the cover of night, avoid the usual paths, and trust no one outside this room," he said with a steely resolve.

Joseph, the former detective, nodded in agreement. "We need to think like Heinz, anticipate his moves, and stay one step ahead. We've outsmarted him once; we can do it again," he added, his analytical mind already sifting through possible strategies.

Magda pulled out a small radio, the group's lifeline to the outside world, and tuned it to a frequency used by the resistance. The static crackled before a voice broke through, updating them on Allied movements and safe zones being established as the front lines shifted.

The briefing concluded with a renewed sense of purpose. Plans were made to send scouts to gather intelligence, ration supplies were distributed, and shifts were set up to keep watch for any signs of the approaching enemy. The group understood that complacency was a luxury they could not afford; vigilance was their watchword.

As they dispersed to their assigned tasks, a quiet camaraderie filled the cabin. They were a band of survivors bound by their shared past and their collective hope for a future free from the shadow of the swastika. And though Oberst Heinz's net was drawing tighter, their resolve to evade capture and to someday bear witness to the world about the horrors they had endured only grew stronger.

With each passing day, the group's legend grew, becoming a whispered symbol of defiance against the Nazi regime, an enduring tale of courage in the face of despair. And within the walls of the cabin in the woods, the seeds of their eventual triumph over adversity were sown, nurtured by the unity and determination of those who had lost everything but each other.

"We'll provide you with new identities, supplies, and a safe route to neutral territory," she assured them.

The group, overwhelmed by gratitude, could hardly believe their luck. But they knew they couldn't afford to let their guard down. The journey ahead was long and fraught with danger.

Karl, pulling Elsie aside, gazed deeply into her eyes. "All those days in the camp, the only thing that kept me going was the thought of us, of a future together," he confessed, his voice thick with emotion. "Promise me, Elsie, that no matter what lies ahead, we'll face it together."

Elsie, tears streaming down her face, nodded. "Always," she vowed.

The group, revitalized and with a renewed sense of purpose, prepared for the next leg of their journey. The road to freedom was still long, but with the strength of their bond and the support of newfound allies, they were ready to face any challenge. And for Elsie and Karl, every step taken was a step closer to a life they had only dared to dream of.

The group made their way through the dense forest, guided only by the stars and their unwavering determination. The path ahead was fraught with danger, but they had taken the first step towards freedom. And for Karl and Elsie, reunited against all odds, the promise of a future together was worth any risk.

11

SACRIFICE AND SURVIVAL

The morning sun, golden and radiant, painted the forest in hues of amber and bronze. But its beauty was lost on Elsie, Karl, and the group of escapees. Their every thought was consumed by the task at hand – reaching the rumoured safe house.

Elsie's heart raced as they moved swiftly through the dense underbrush. Every rustle of leaves, every snap of a twig, was magnified in her heightened state of alertness. She clung to Karl's hand, drawing strength from his unwavering presence.

The path was treacherous. Markus, with his innate sense of direction, led the way, guiding them through hidden trails and obscure routes. But as the day wore on, a nagging sensation tugged at the edges of his consciousness – the feeling of being watched.

His fears were confirmed when Anya, her keen eyes darting around, signalled for the group to halt. From their vantage point atop a small ridge, she had spotted a patrol of Nazi soldiers, their distinctive uniforms unmistakable even from a distance. They were methodically combing the forest, their search patterns indicating they were closing in on the group's trail.

A heavy silence descended upon the escapees, the gravity of their situation sinking in. They were trapped, the soldiers on one side and a vast, treacherous river on the other. Crossing it would be dangerous, if not impossible. Yet, staying put meant capture or worse.

It was Markus who broke the silence. "We need a diversion," he declared, his voice steady. "Something to draw them away, to give the rest of you a fighting chance."

Anya nodded in agreement. "If a few of us can lead them on a wild goose chase, the rest can make for the safe house."

The group was torn. The plan was sound but fraught with danger. Who would stay behind? Who would make the ultimate sacrifice for the others?

Elsie, her heart heavy, stepped forward. "I'll do it," she whispered, determination shining in her eyes. Karl, horrified, tried to protest, but she silenced him with a tender kiss. "Remember our promise," she murmured, tears streaming down her face. "To find freedom, to find peace."

Karl, torn between his love for Elsie and the reality of their situation, finally nodded, his eyes filled with a raw pain. "Be safe," he whispered, pulling her into a tight embrace.

With heavy hearts and a final, lingering look at their loved ones, the four set off, drawing the soldiers' attention and leading them away from the main group.

In the dense woods bordering the cabin, Elsie and her group hatched a plan for a daring diversion. The objective was clear: to draw the Nazi forces away long enough for the main group of escapees to slip through the net Oberst Heinz was drawing ever tighter.

They decided on a two-pronged approach to create chaos and confusion. The first part of their plan involved setting a series of controlled fires. They chose a location far enough from their hideout to avoid detection but close enough to the main roads that it would draw attention. They worked in pairs, moving stealthily through the underbrush, setting small, smoldering fires designed to erupt into flames at staggered intervals, creating the illusion of a large, disorganized band of partisans moving through the area.

The second part of their plan was to stage a mock skirmish. Joseph, with his experience as a detective, had meticulously gathered uniforms and weapons from fallen Nazi soldiers over the previous months. The group donned these uniforms and staged a firefight in a clearing, complete with the sound of blank rounds and explosive charges set to mimic grenades.

This mock battle was designed to be heard by a nearby patrol, leading them to believe a significant resistance force was engaging in the area. With the fires as a visible signal and the sounds of gunfire as an audible one, the ruse was set to unfold.

As the fires began to catch and spread, painting the night sky with ominous glows, the group initiated the false firefight. The sounds of their 'battle' echoed through the woods, and as expected, it wasn't long before the distant shouts of Nazi patrols and the sounds of vehicles moving rapidly could be heard. They had taken the bait.

Elsie and the others maintained the ruse long enough to ensure the patrols were fully committed to their response. Once the Nazi forces were focused on the diversion, the group used pre-dug foxholes and tunnels to disappear into the forest, leaving behind a scene chaotic enough to keep the enemy occupied with sorting truth from fiction.

As the Nazi forces converged on the site of the fires and the supposed skirmish, Elsie's group retreated to a secondary rendezvous point. Their hearts pounded not just from exertion but from the adrenaline of having played their parts in a dangerous but necessary deception.

This diversion, crafted with ingenuity and executed with precision, was a testament to the courage and resourcefulness of those who refused to bow under the yoke of tyranny. It was a small victory in the larger war, but for those involved, it was a profound affirmation of their agency in a world that sought to strip them of it.

The sounds of gunfire and shouts echoed in the distance, providing the rest with the window of opportunity they desperately needed. Karl, with Anya by his side, led the remainder of the group towards the safe house.

Hours turned into days, the journey fraught with danger at every turn. But, against all odds, they reached their destination. Tucked away in a secluded grove surrounded by the dense forest, the safe house was a modest cottage, its appearance deliberately unremarkable to avoid drawing any unwanted attention. Its weathered wooden exterior, covered in climbing ivy, blended seamlessly with the verdant landscape, and the thick thatched roof provided natural insulation against both the cold and the prying ears of aerial reconnaissance.

Upon arrival, the group was greeted by a resistance member known to them only by his code name, "Sokół," the Polish word for falcon. His sharp eyes and alert demeanor embodied the bird he was named after. A trusted operative within the resistance, he was part of a larger network that had helped many others like Elsie and Karl evade capture.

"Sokół," born Tomasz Nowak in the vibrant heart of Kraków, was a man whose life had become irrevocably intertwined with the fate of his country. The son of a teacher and a nurse, Sokół's early years were steeped in academia and a strong sense of national pride. His youth was punctuated by the echoes of Chopin's nocturnes and the passionate discussions of Poland's storied history and culture.

When Poland was cleaved in two by the Molotov-Ribbentrop Pact, Sokół's fiery patriotism transformed into action. He joined the underground resistance movement, his keen intellect and linguistic skills making him an invaluable asset. As Poland was ravaged by war, Sokół became a courier, slipping through the shadows, delivering messages and coordinating with other cells.

His activities led to several close calls with the Gestapo, and each escape only honed his skills and resolve. The nom de guerre "Sokół" was bestowed upon him by his compatriots, inspired by his ability to elude capture with the acumen and agility of a falcon.

When the Warsaw Uprising shattered the heart of his beloved city, Sokół was among the brave who fought and survived. The crushing defeat did not break his spirit; instead, it galvanized his determination to aid those in the crosshairs of the Nazi regime.

By the time Karl, along with the others, arrived at the cottage, Sokół had already orchestrated numerous successful operations. His life, once defined by scholarly pursuits, had become a testament to the indomitable will of the Polish resistance—a life dedicated to the liberation of his people and his homeland.

Sokół ushered them inside where they were introduced to the rest of the resistance cell operating the safe house. There was Marta, a stern but kind woman who served as the medic.

Marta Kowalska's journey to the safe house was a tale of resilience and profound courage. Born in 1908 in the pastoral tranquility of Podhale, Poland's southernmost region, Marta grew up in the shadow of the Tatra Mountains, in a world where tradition and community were the bedrock of life. Her mother was a midwife, and from her, Marta inherited a deep compassion for others and a deft skill in caring for the sick.

When she moved to Warsaw for nursing school, Marta's world expanded. The bustling city introduced her to a myriad of ideas and people, but the pull of her mountain home remained strong. She returned to Podhale as a qualified nurse, determined to serve her community.

However, the outbreak of World War II shattered the peaceful life Marta had known. When the Wehrmacht stormed through Poland, the horrors of war followed in their wake. Marta witnessed the suffering of her countrymen and realized that her role as a healer was needed now more than ever.

As the occupation grew more oppressive, Marta's resolve hardened. She became part of the underground resistance, her medical knowledge proving invaluable. She tended to wounded partisans, delivered medicines to those in hiding, and provided covert care to Jews escaping the ghettos. Her home became a secret sanctuary, her hands a source of healing amid the brutality of war.

The Gestapo's net was always closing in, and Marta was forced to flee her beloved mountains to continue her work. She moved from place to place, always one step ahead of capture, her name whispered reverently among the resistance as a symbol of hope.

Marta's role in the safe house was pivotal. She was the medic, the caretaker, the steady hand in a world upturned. Her presence was a balm to the weary souls who found refuge within the cottage's walls. She listened to their stories, wiped away their tears, and patched their wounds, both seen and unseen.

Her past, a tapestry of care in the face of fear, had led her to this point. Within the safety of the forest hideaway, Marta continued to fight the only way she knew how—by preserving life in a time filled with death.

She had turned one of the rooms into a makeshift infirmary, its shelves lined with jars of herbs and medical supplies, which she had miraculously managed to procure.

Then there was Michał, the group's radio operator. Michał Wojciechowski's life before the war was one of quiet scholarship and technological fascination. Born in 1910 in the industrious city of Łódź, Poland, to a family of textile workers, Michał's keen interest in radio technology set him apart from an early age. His father, a man of practical skills, recognized his son's intellectual talents and scrimped and saved to send Michał to the University of Warsaw to study engineering.

In the electrifying academic environment of the 1930s, Michał thrived, his natural aptitude for electrical systems and communications technology quickly earning him the respect of his professors and peers. His passion for amateur radio, an exciting and rapidly developing field, soon became both a hobby and an obsession. He spent long nights huddled over his homemade radio set, communicating with people from distant lands, marveling at the power of invisible waves to connect the world.

But as the political climate in Europe soured and war clouds gathered, Michał's skills took on a new significance. When Poland was invaded in 1939, his world changed overnight. The university was shuttered, and the city occupied. Michał returned to Łódź, only to find his family's home commandeered by German soldiers.

Refusing to succumb to despair, Michał's expertise in radio technology found a new purpose in the resistance movement. His ability to build and repair radio transmitters became invaluable to the underground networks that sprang up in the wake of occupation. Operating under the radar of the Nazi regime, he became a linchpin in the communication chain that connected the fragmented pockets of Polish resistance.

His clandestine activities were not without risk, and Michał became a master of evasion. He learned to encode messages, to vary transmission times and frequencies, always staying one step ahead of the German efforts to jam or trace his signals. He was forced to move frequently, each new location a temporary haven until suspicion or danger grew too close.

The war took its toll on Michał, as it did on all who lived through those times. Friends were lost, and the vibrant cityscapes of his youth were reduced to rubble. But through it all, he never lost his resolve. The radio waves that he had once used for leisurely international chat became the threads that held together the fabric of the resistance, and he wove these threads with unwavering dedication.

By the time he became the radio operator at the cottage safe house, Michał had become more than an engineer or a hobbyist; he was a lifeline, a beacon of hope that kept the fight alive, broadcasting whispers of freedom through the crackling airwaves of a continent at war.

His equipment was hidden in a concealed cellar beneath the cottage, accessible by a trapdoor under the kitchen table. Michał was in constant contact with other resistance cells and the Allied forces, gathering intelligence and coordinating movements.

The heart of the cottage was its hearth, where a sturdy, cast-iron stove provided warmth and served as the communal cooking area.

Here, Anna, a former chef from Warsaw, worked her magic with the limited rations, turning them into meals that nourished the body and soul.

Anna Zielinski's story was as rich and layered as the dishes she so lovingly prepared. Born in 1914 into the vibrant heart of Gdańsk, a port city where Polish and German cultures intermingled, Anna's childhood was infused with a love of food. Her father was a fisherman, braving the Baltic Sea to provide for his family, while her mother ran a modest but popular eatery where locals and travelers alike savored her hearty, home-cooked meals.

From an early age, Anna was her mother's sous chef, learning the delicate balance of spices, the patience required for perfect dough, and the rhythms of a kitchen in full swing. Her mother's belief that food was more than sustenance—it was a language of care, community, and culture—became Anna's creed.

When the war broke out and Gdańsk was engulfed in conflict, Anna's world turned upside down. Her family eatery was destroyed in a bombing raid, and her father was lost at sea. With her mother and siblings, Anna fled the only home she'd ever known, eventually settling in Warsaw. It was there, amid the war's chaos, that Anna found her calling in the resistance.

Her skills in the kitchen became an unexpected asset. Anna cooked for meetings held in concealed basements, her unassuming appearance allowing her to move through the city unnoticed, carrying messages and plans hidden in food baskets. Her restaurant, a modest establishment on the outskirts of Warsaw, became a hub for clandestine operations, its tables a front for the exchange of covert intelligence.

But as the grip of the Gestapo tightened, Anna's activities drew dangerous attention. A close call with an informant forced her to abandon her beloved Warsaw, leaving behind the remnants of her family restaurant and the city that had become her second home.

In the resistance network, Anna's reputation for courage and warmth preceded her. When she arrived at the safe house, deep in the cover of Poland's forests, she was embraced as both a comrade and a lifeline. Here, she transformed meager rations into meals that nourished hearts and fortified spirits. The kitchen became her domain, a place of comfort and normalcy amidst the uncertainty of war.

As she cooked, Anna would share stories of Gdańsk's bustling markets, of the flavors that once danced upon the city's air, and of the family she'd lost and the resilience they'd instilled in her. For the group of weary escapees, Anna's meals and memories became a reminder of the world they were fighting to preserve—a world where freedom and fellowship sat at the same table.

Her laughter and the aroma of her cooking filled the cottage, lending a semblance of normalcy to their fraught existence.

The cottage was strategically chosen for its location, which was not only hidden but also equidistant from several escape routes should an emergency evacuation become necessary. It was fortified discreetly, with false walls for hiding and a well-concealed observation post in the attic that provided a panoramic view of the surrounding area.

Though the space was cramped, with makeshift bedding arranged in the common area at night, it was a sanctuary compared to the horrors they had endured. The camaraderie within the walls of the safe house was palpable, a shared understanding among people who had seen too much yet refused to give up hope.

In this humble abode, strategy sessions were held around the dining table, plans were drawn in hushed tones, and friendships were forged in the firelight. It was a place where weary souls found rest, where battle plans were devised, and where the flickering flame of resistance continued to burn bright.

Yet, amidst the relative safety, Karl's heart was heavy. Every night, he would step outside, gazing at the vast expanse of the night sky, praying for a sign, a glimmer of hope that Elsie was safe.

Days turned into weeks, and with no word from Elsie or Markus, despair began to take root. The group mourned their loss, each grappling with the weight of their sacrifice.

It was on one such evening, as Karl sat by the window, lost in thought, that a soft knock echoed through the silence. The door creaked open to reveal a weary, battered Elsie, her eyes reflecting the horrors she had witnessed but shining with an indomitable spirit.

The reunion was tearful and heartfelt. Elsie recounted her ordeal. "The labyrinth of my escape was paved with fear and uncertainty, a patchwork of near misses and split-second decisions that could have meant the difference between life and death. It was a journey marked not by the miles traveled but by the countless moments when fate seemed to teeter on a knife-edge.

Markus and I, along with a small group of fellow fugitives, had woven our way through the countryside, navigating by the stars and the whispered guidance of allies in the resistance. We traversed fields under the cover of night, skirted the edges of towns where the loyal eyes of the regime were ever-watchful, and sought refuge in the shadows of barns and forests.

On one particularly fraught evening, as we sought passage across a checkpoint that was rumored to be lightly guarded, we found ourselves face-to-face with a patrol. Our hearts sank as the soldiers approached, their faces stern in the dim glow of their flashlights. It was then that Anya, a woman of fierce spirit and quick wit, feigned a fainting spell, collapsing onto the cold ground. The soldiers, momentarily distracted by her plight, loosened their vigilance just enough for Markus to subtly signal me. In the ensuing commotion, as the soldiers debated what to do, we slipped away, like shadows dissolving into the night.

We had close calls, too many to count. Once, as we hid in the musty loft of an old mill, the grinding halt of a German military truck outside sent chills down our spines. We could hear the soldiers' boots on the wooden floor below, the harsh cadence of their voices. We lay as still as death, pressed into the rough grain of the floorboards, as the search below grew increasingly fervent. I remember the dust motes dancing in the slats of light, the smell of mold and old grain, and the sound of my own breath, which I feared was too loud.

It was Markus's calmness, his unerring sense of timing, that saw us through each encounter. When to hide, when to run, when to blend in with a crowd—his instincts were unerring. But it wasn't just his actions that saved us; it was the sacrifices of others, those brave souls who chose to create diversions, who offered us their hiding places, who sometimes got caught in our stead.

I recall a young couple, resistance fighters who had harbored us in the cellar of their home. When the Gestapo came knocking, it was they who claimed our forged papers as their own, leading the suspicion away from us. We left that night to the sound of boots on wooden floors and muffled voices, knowing in our hearts the price of our continued freedom might be their lives.

These threads of humanity, woven through the dark tapestry of war, sustained me. The kindness of a farmer who hid us in his hayloft, the courage of a priest who smuggled us past a checkpoint in his humble cart, the solidarity of a shopkeeper who passed a loaf of bread into our trembling hands with a nod of understanding—they were beacons of hope in a world gone mad.

And when I finally saw Karl again, when I stepped into the safety of the cabin and into the circle of his arms, the relief was indescribable. The pain, fear, and loss we had endured seemed to dissolve for a moment. In his embrace, I found not just solace but a renewed sense of purpose. We had been hunted, we had been haunted, but we had not been broken. Our story, like that of so many others, was one of resilience—a testament to the enduring strength of the human spirit."

The two, wrapped in each other's arms, gazing out at the horizon. The world outside might still be chaotic, filled with danger and uncertainty, but in that moment, all that mattered was their shared love and the sacrifices they had made to be together. The journey ahead was still long, but with each other by their side, they were ready to face whatever the future held.

The nights at the safe house were filled with hushed whispers and shared stories. The group, drawn together by their shared experiences and the pain of their losses, became an ad-hoc family. The warmth of the fireplace became their focal point, around which tales of heroism, love, and hope were shared.

Anya, still reeling from the sacrifices made for their escape, took it upon herself to document their stories. She believed that the world needed to know, that future generations should understand the depths of their resilience and the heights of the atrocities they'd faced.

Markus, on the other hand, channelled his energy into ensuring their safety. The safe house, while secluded, was still vulnerable. He set about creating hidden exits, traps, and vantage points. The resistance provided them with information and updates, and it became clear that while the immediate threat had subsided, they were far from truly safe.

One evening, as the group gathered for dinner, a knock resounded through the stillness. It was a code – three short, two long – the sign of a trusted member of the resistance. The door opened to reveal a middle-aged man, his face lined with fatigue but eyes burning with a fierce determination.

He introduced himself as Lukasz, a high-ranking member of the Polish resistance.

Born in 1905 in Warsaw, Poland, Lukasz Nowak hailed from a lineage of Polish nationalists. The Nowak family, proud of their heritage, had a history of resisting any foreign domination, from the partitions of Poland in the 18th century to the more recent occupations in the 20th century.

Lukasz was a prodigious child, both in terms of intellect and physical abilities. As a teenager, he excelled in academics, but his passion lay in fencing and horseback riding, activities that would later serve him well. He studied political science at the University of Warsaw, where he was exposed to various nationalist ideologies and movements.

When Poland regained its independence in 1918 after 123 years of partitions, a young Lukasz dreamt of a progressive, self-sufficient nation. He began his career in the civil service but always maintained close ties with various Polish nationalist groups.

However, the invasion of Poland in 1939 by Germany and the Soviet Union deeply affected Lukasz. The devastation of his beloved Warsaw in the subsequent bombings, and the loss of many of his close friends and family, ignited a fire within him. He couldn't stand idly by as his country was torn apart.

Utilizing his extensive contacts within the military and civil sectors, Lukasz became a founding member of the "Armie Krajowa" or the Home Army, which was the dominant Polish resistance movement during World War II. Due to his charisma, strategic acumen, and relentless spirit, he quickly rose to become a high-ranking member.

Lukasz was instrumental in organizing covert operations against the Nazi occupiers. From sabotage missions that disrupted German supply lines to gathering crucial intelligence for the Allies, he was at the forefront. But perhaps his most significant contribution was aiding Jews in their escape and establishing safe routes and havens for them. Despite the immense risks, Lukasz believed in the fundamental principle of humanity above all else.

However, his activities didn't go unnoticed. The Gestapo had a significant bounty on his head, and he was often on the move, evading capture using a series of aliases and disguises. But Lukasz wasn't just running; he was always planning, always strategizing.

He had news – and a proposal.

"The Nazis," he began, his voice grim, "are intensifying their search. They've begun raiding known safe houses. We've lost many."

The room was heavy with tension, the weight of his words sinking in.

"But," Lukasz continued, "there's a way out. We've secured a route that leads to the Swiss border. It's treacherous, but it's our best shot."

Elsie and Karl exchanged a glance, their decision made in that fleeting moment of shared understanding. They would take the risk. The dream of a life beyond the shadows of war, of a place where their love could thrive unburdened, was too alluring to pass up.

The next few days were a blur of preparations. Maps were studied, supplies gathered, and roles assigned. The group, once bound by their shared trauma, was now united in their singular goal – freedom.

The night of their departure was moonless, the darkness their only ally. Lukasz led the way, his knowledge of the terrain proving invaluable. They navigated dense forests, crossed treacherous rivers, and evaded Nazi patrols with a mix of luck and skill.

But as they neared the border, disaster struck. A sudden ambush caught them off guard. Gunfire echoed through the night, and chaos ensued. Lukasz, with a cry of warning, was hit, his body crumpling to the ground. The group scattered, each seeking cover, the dream of freedom suddenly hanging by a thread.

In the heat of the moment, Karl and Elsie were separated. Desperate shouts were drowned by the deafening gunfire. Elsie, hiding behind a fallen log, caught a glimpse of Karl, pinned down by enemy fire.

With a surge of adrenaline, she made a choice. Grabbing a nearby branch, she charged at the nearest soldier, catching him off guard. The distraction was enough. Karl, seizing the opportunity, managed to break free, taking down two soldiers in the process.

But their victory was short-lived. A sudden, sharp pain shot through Elsie's leg, and she fell, a bullet having found its mark. Karl, his heart filled with terror, rushed to her side, cradling her.

The sounds of the skirmish faded as the remaining members of their group, using the diversion, overwhelmed the soldiers. The immediate threat was neutralized, but the damage was done.

As dawn broke, the group found themselves on the Swiss border, the promise of safety just beyond the rolling hills ahead. But the cost was high. Elsie, pale and weak, was carried on an improvised stretcher, her fate uncertain.

Karl, tears streaming down his face, held onto Elsie's hand as they cross into Switzerland. The landscape, serene and picturesque, stands in stark contrast to the pain and sacrifices of their journey. Their love, tested by the harshest of trials, remains unbroken, a beacon of hope in a world torn apart by war.

12

AFTERMATH

The bells tolled across the land, resonating with an exultation that swept from village to city, crossing boundaries and uniting hearts. World War II had finally come to an end. The skies, once darkened by warplanes and filled with the acrid smoke of battle, now gleamed with a newfound hope. But for many, the end of the war was not a simple return to normalcy; it was the beginning of a new struggle – the challenge of piecing together shattered lives.

In a quaint Swiss village, nestled amidst rolling hills and serene lakes, stood a modest house, its wooden facade bearing silent testimony to the stories within. It had been two years since the end of the war, but its shadows lingered. Elsie, her once vibrant spirit subdued, gazed out of the window, the distant mountains reflecting her introspective mood.

Her leg, injured during their harrowing escape, had healed, but not without leaving its mark. She walked with a slight limp, a constant reminder of the price of freedom. But more than the physical scars, it was the emotional ones that weighed her down.

Karl, returning from the village market, watched her from the doorway. The vivacious, fiery woman he had fallen in love with seemed lost, trapped in memories they both wished they could forget. The trauma of Auschwitz, the looming presence of Oberst Heinz, and the pain of their escape had taken a toll.

"Thinking about the past again?" Karl asked gently, placing a hand on her shoulder.

Elsie sighed, her gaze still fixed on the horizon. "Sometimes I wonder if we'll ever truly be free, Karl. The war is over, but its echoes remain."

Karl nodded, understanding her sentiment. "We've been through unimaginable horrors, Elsie. But we have each other, and we have this moment. We must learn to live in the present."

Elsie turned to face him, her eyes shimmering with unshed tears. "I love you, Karl, but sometimes I fear that our love was a product of the circumstances. In the camp, amidst all that despair, we clung to each other. But now, in the real world, can our love survive?"

Karl, taken aback, took a moment to gather his thoughts. "Our love was born in adversity, true. But it's not defined by it. We've shared dreams, hopes, fears – not just as prisoners, but as two souls intertwined."

The days that followed were a whirlwind of emotions. The couple, grappling with their shared trauma, sought solace in different ways. Elsie, ever the nurturer, began volunteering at a local orphanage, finding purpose in caring for children scarred by the war. Karl, on the other hand, threw himself into writing, penning down their experiences, turning pain into prose.

But despite their individual pursuits, a distance grew between them. The once inseparable pair found themselves drifting, their bond tested by the mundanities of daily life.

One evening, as a storm raged outside, the tensions reached a breaking point. Accusations were hurled, tears shed, and for a moment, it seemed like their love story, which had weathered so much, was on the brink of collapse.

Elsie, her voice shaking, finally uttered the words that had been haunting her. "Maybe we were never meant to be, Karl. Maybe we were just two souls seeking comfort in a cruel world."

Karl, his heart heavy, replied, "Elsie, our love was never just about the camp. It was about us, about finding light in the darkest of times. But if you truly believe we're better apart, I'll respect your decision."

The night was long and fraught with uncertainty. But as dawn broke, a realization dawned on Elsie. Their love was not a mere byproduct of their circumstances; it was a testament to their resilience. They had built something beautiful from the ashes of their pain, and it was worth fighting for.

She approached Karl, who was lost in thought by the window, and whispered, "I was wrong. Our love is real, and I want to fight for it."

Karl, turning to face her, took her into his arms, sealing their commitment with a kiss.

The couple, hand in hand, watch the sunrise, its golden rays symbolic of a new beginning. The war was over, and while its scars would never truly fade, their love remained – a beacon of hope, a testament to the indomitable human spirit.

As the weeks turned into months, the quaint Swiss village became the backdrop for their healing. Elsie and Karl, once divided by their internal conflicts, now consciously invested time in understanding each other outside the traumatic confines of their shared past.

It began with small gestures: Karl reading excerpts from his writings to Elsie, opening a window into his mind; Elsie bringing home stories from the orphanage, sharing the joy and heartbreaks of the children she was growing to love. Through these exchanges, they not only rediscovered each other but also started seeing their own reflections more clearly.

One evening, they organized a small gathering at their home. Friends from the resistance, neighbours from the village, and a few familiar faces from Auschwitz came together. The night was filled with music, dance, laughter, and shared stories. It was a testament to their journey, from victims of war to survivors and pillars of strength for others. For many attendees, it was the first time they laughed or danced since the war's end.

During the gathering, Anya approached Elsie with a small package. "I found this during one of our resistance missions," she whispered, handing it over. Unwrapping it, Elsie found a photo of herself from before the war – young, carefree, and radiant.

"It's a reminder," Anya said, her voice choked with emotion. "A reminder of who you were, who you became, and the incredible strength you carry within."

Elsie, tears in her eyes, hugged Anya. The photograph wasn't just an image; it was a bridge between her past and present, a symbol of resilience.

As the evening came to a close, Karl took centre stage, his harmonica in hand. Playing a soulful tune, he beckoned Elsie to join him. The two danced, lost in each other, their movements telling a story more profound than words ever could. Those watching were entranced, witnessing not just a dance but a celebration of love that had survived against all odds.

The next morning, the house was filled with a tranquil silence. Elsie and Karl, over breakfast, made a decision. They would establish a refuge in the village, a haven for survivors of the war. It would be a place of healing, of understanding, where shattered souls could find peace and purpose.

Using their experiences, they began to weave together a community. Workshops, therapy sessions, and communal gatherings became regular events. Survivors from all walks of life began to trickle in, finding solace in shared experiences and the promise of a brighter tomorrow.

Elsie and Karl stood in front of their refuge, its doors open to a world scarred by war but not devoid of hope. Their love, once fragile and tested, had not only endured but had become the foundation for countless others' healing journeys. They had emerged from the depths of despair, proving that even in the aftermath of the darkest storms, love and hope could thrive.

The years rolled on, bringing with them the challenges of age and health. But Elsie and Karl, having weathered the harshest of storms, faced each obstacle with grace and unity.

Elsie's later years were spent in the tranquility of a world at peace, a stark contrast to the one she had survived. She often sat in her garden, surrounded by flowers and the photographs of those she had loved and lost, reflecting on the past with a heart full of gratitude for the present.

As she aged, Elsie became a beacon in her community, a wise elder whose resilience inspired those around her. When she passed, peacefully and surrounded by loved ones, her passing was mourned not only by those who knew her but also by those who knew of her—a woman who had turned the shadows of her life into solace for millions.

Years later, an elderly Karl, penned their story, ensuring that their tale of love, sacrifice, and resilience would live on. Beside him, a photograph of a young, radiant Elsie, taken before the war, stands as a testament to their enduring bond. Through the highs and lows, shadows and solace, their love remained, a beacon of hope in a world that had once known so much despair.

13

THE DESCENT OF OBERST HEINZ

The escape of Elsie and Karl was a black mark on Oberst Heinz's otherwise relentless reign of terror in Auschwitz. To him, it wasn't just a mere escape; it was a direct challenge to his authority, an open mockery of his power. Furious and humiliated, he ordered an immediate crackdown on the camp's inmates, believing it would snuff out any remnants of hope or resistance. But in truth, he had lost a significant chunk of his formidable aura, and whispers of his 'failure' echoed among both prisoners and guards.

In the chaotic last days of the war, as the Allies closed in, there was a desperate scramble within the Nazi regime. Documents were destroyed, evidence buried, and an effort was made to eliminate any traces of the Holocaust's horrors. Oberst Heinz, ever the opportunist, saw a chance to reinvent himself. He began to secretly gather and hoard valuable items stolen from the prisoners, planning an escape to a non-extradition country with his ill-gotten wealth.

However, fate had other plans. In his attempt to flee, he was captured by a group of Polish partisans. Recognizing him immediately, they handed him over to the advancing Soviet forces, ensuring he'd face the justice he so richly deserved.

Heinz was transported to Moscow, where he underwent a series of intense interrogations. The once proud and fearsome commandant was reduced to a shell, often breaking down, oscillating between self-pity and defiant proclamations of innocence. The Soviets, having documented testimonies of his brutalities, prepared for his trial.

The Nuremberg Trials were in full swing, and Oberst Heinz was among the high-profile figures to be tried. As he stood in the dock, the grandiosity of the courtroom was in stark contrast to the man himself. Gone was the intimidating aura, replaced by a palpable sense of fear and apprehension.

The testimonies against him were overwhelming. Survivors recounted tales of his brutalities, with some even producing clandestine sketches and notes detailing his actions. The most damning evidence came in the form of records meticulously maintained by his own administration, detailing executions, torture methods, and other atrocities.

However, it was the testimony of Elsie and Karl that proved to be the most impactful. Their harrowing recount of their time in Auschwitz, combined with their eventual escape, painted a vivid picture of Heinz's sadism. The courtroom, which had heard countless tales of horror, was moved to silence by their words.

Heinz's defense was weak and often contradictory. He tried to distance himself from the atrocities, laying the blame on subordinates and even suggesting that he had been a silent resistor to the regime's actions. But the evidence was irrefutable.

As the trial reached its climax, a psychiatrist was called upon to evaluate Heinz. The report painted a picture of a deeply disturbed individual, a sociopath who revelled in the power he wielded and showed no genuine remorse for his actions. The man who once held the power of life and death over thousands was clinically dissected, his psyche laid bare for the world to see.

The verdict was unanimous: guilty on all counts. Oberst Heinz was sentenced to death. His final days were spent in a small, dimly lit cell, a far cry from his commandant quarters in Auschwitz. The gravity of his situation finally seemed to dawn on him. Guards reported hearing him weep at night, his cries echoing in the silent corridors.

The day of his execution drew a significant crowd. There was a palpable tension in the air, a mix of relief and anticipation. As he was led to the gallows, a hush fell over the gathered masses. With the drop of the platform, the chapter of Oberst Heinz came to a definitive close.

In the aftermath, as Europe tried to rebuild and come to terms with the war's horrors, Heinz's name became synonymous with the cruelty of the Holocaust. His story served as a grim reminder of the depths humanity could sink to and the importance of never forgetting the lessons of history.

In the years that followed, the legacy of Oberst Heinz's brutality lived on, not just as a dark chapter in history books, but as a haunting memory in the minds of Auschwitz survivors. As they scattered across the globe, establishing new lives in various countries, their tales about the cruel commandant remained consistent. Their stories served as a chilling testament, ensuring future generations understood the depths of inhumanity that had occurred.

Elsie, in her subsequent years, took it upon herself to be a voice for those who couldn't speak. Alongside Karl, they travelled to schools, universities, and various institutions, recounting their personal experiences. During one of these sessions, when asked about Oberst Heinz, Elsie remarked, "He was a reflection of the evil that can reside within any society that loses its way, a reminder that we must always be vigilant against the rise of hatred and intolerance."

As for Auschwitz, it transformed from a place of death and despair to a solemn monument for peace and reflection. Every brick, every path, and every barrack bore silent witness to the atrocities that had occurred there. And prominently displayed within its museum was an entire section dedicated to Oberst Heinz, ensuring visitors grasped the pivotal role he played in the camp's grim history.

Historians and scholars analyzed Heinz's rapid rise within the Nazi ranks and his eventual downfall, seeking to understand the psyche of such individuals. Many publications and documentaries were produced, dissecting his character, motives, and actions. Yet, even with all this analysis, a shroud of enigma continued to surround him. The core question remained: Was he a product of a hateful ideology, or did the ideology find a ready vessel in him?

Decades after the war, on the anniversary of Heinz's execution, a ceremony was held at the site of his death. Survivors, their families, and representatives from various nations gathered to commemorate the moment. There was no sense of celebration, no air of victory; instead, there was a heavy atmosphere of reflection. It was a day of mixed emotions—gratitude for the justice served, sorrow for the countless lives lost, and hope for a world where such horrors would never be repeated.

As the sun set, casting long shadows over the gathering, a young girl, a grandchild of one of the survivors, stepped forward. She sang a haunting melody, a lullaby from the pre-war days. Her voice echoed the collective pain, loss, and hope of all those present. And in that moment, the chapter of Oberst Heinz truly felt complete—not with a sense of closure, but with a firm commitment to ensure his kind of evil would never rise again.

Today, Auschwitz Concentration Camp in southern Poland stands as a somber museum, a testament to the Holocaust's horrors. The preserved barracks and haunting remnants of gas chambers bear witness to the atrocities committed. The iconic sign, "Arbeit macht frei," still marks the entrance, while memorial stones honour the myriad lives lost.

Don't miss out!

Visit the website below and you can sign up to receive emails whenever Blake Patrick publishes a new book. There's no charge and no obligation.

https://books2read.com/r/B-A-DEZBB-DEWRC

Connecting independent readers to independent writers.

Also by Blake Patrick

Chronicles of the Eternal Nile
Whispers of the Nile

The RIP Squad Chronicles
Pendle's Curse

Standalone
Fractured Shields
Hidden Cargo
Shadow of a Witch
Shadows and Solace
Whispered Promises